Lady in Distress

"Miss Armstrong, you are the most rag-mannered female I know! It is clear now that you are no picture of innocence wronged, no diminished virtue come to demand retribution. Don't come to me with your self-righteous little nose in the air."

That same little nose was starting to sniffle. Some truths hurt, but broken dreams hurt worse. She was weeping now.

The Earl mopped his forehead with his hankerchief, then quickly handed it to Noelle. "Please, Miss Armstrong, please sit and...and I'll call for tea. Why don't you take a moment to compose yourself." The Earl knew exactly how to deal with a lady in distress: throw water on her, call for a maid or kiss her. But the situation did not look desperate enough for water, there was no maid, and the Earl had an inkling he would get slapped if he followed his own inclination...

Other Avon Books by
Barbara Metzger

BETHING'S FOLLY

THE EARL
AND THE HEIRESS

BARBARA METZGER

AVON
PUBLISHERS OF BARD, CAMELOT, DISCUS AND FLARE BOOKS

All the characters and events portrayed in this story are fictitious.

AVON BOOKS
A division of
The Hearst Corporation
1790 Broadway
New York, New York 10019

Copyright © 1982 by Barbara Metzger
Published by arrangement with Walker and Company, Inc.
Library of Congress Catalog Card Number: 82-70760
ISBN: 0-380-65516-0

First Avon Printing, December, 1983

Printed in the U.S.A.

WFH 10 9 8 7 6 5 4 3 2 1

*To Diogenes Jim
and
J.I.M.
two of the best friends
a girl ever had*

=== 1 ===

MISS ARMSTRONG'S ASSETS

WHEN AN AUNT travels on to her just rewards, it is natural and fitting for a niece to mourn her passing. When it is a great-aunt who has departed, however, an ancient lady of a crotchety, curmudgeonly disposition, then it is difficult to maintain the proper degree of grief, especially when the aunt had never forgiven your mother for marrying the handsome rake who was your father, nor refrained from enumerating his sins at every opportunity. And when, finally, the old harridan names you, her eldest niece, as heiress to her London town house and a small competence, propriety be damned!

"Champagne, Win," called Miss Noelle Armstrong to her younger brother Winston, Viscount Sterling. "Go find us some champagne. We're going to London!"

She grabbed her younger sister Ferne's hands and started a mad dance around the shabby drawing-room furniture to a chorus of "London Bridge is falling down, my fair Nellie." The two girls skipped around the worn sofa where their Aunt Hattie was searching in her workbasket for her spectacles, so she might read the solicitor's letter over to herself, the better to believe it. A tiny white dog leaped off the sofa and ran, barking, to a basket near the fireplace where another just like it, and just like an animated dust mop, also sat barking, avoiding the commotion, perhaps, or adding to it. Quiet did not come to the small parlour until Winston returned with a tray.

"No champagne, Nellie, but Mrs. Strubbing found us some of Papa's old sherry. It will have to do."

"Perfect, Winnie. Papa would be very glad." Noelle poured out the wine and passed the glasses. When everyone was served she raised hers, saying, "I would like to propose a toast. To

Great-aunt Sylvia, may she rest in peace." There was a whispered "Amen" from Ferne and an "Oh dear, I don't think that's quite the thing" from Aunt Hattie, but before anyone could taste the sherry, Noelle continued: "And to a Season in London, with balls and the Theatre and bookstores."

"And card parties," put in Aunt Hattie.

"Tattersall's," from Winston, and "New dresses, mightn't we?" softly from seventeen-year-old Ferne.

"Hear, hear!" Winston tipped his glass up and quaffed the whole with all the maturity of his twenty years, while the ladies sipped. His choking almost drowned out Ferne's gasp, whether for the unexpected warmth in her throat, or the awful thought that had just entered her beautiful blond head.

"Nellie," she asked, "must we wear black? I couldn't bear going to London in mourning and not being able to dance." Her unhappy eyes seemed even larger and bluer than usual, making her resemble a Renaissance angel more than ever.

Noelle turned in dismay to her aunt, who had once actually lived in London and who was, therefore, the Armstrongs' only arbiter of Town ways.

"Why, no." Aunt Hattie deliberated. "The solicitor writes that Sylvia died some months past. She was on one of her jaunts, to Turkistan or some outlandish place, I assume, hence the delay in notifying us. The London Season does not start for some few months still, and by then only the highest sticklers would expect half-mourning. This family has seen quite enough black as it is; it is high time you got out and enjoyed yourselves. Besides, you children hardly knew Sylvia Wycombe." Hattie poured herself another glass of wine and drank it, muttering something that sounded suspiciously like "Your better luck."

Sharing her sofa, Winston was the only one to hear. He grinned. "I don't believe I saw her more than twice. She said I was a nasty, dirty little boy, and I looked just like papa, as though one was as bad as the other. But you must have known her better, Nell. After all, she did leave you her money."

Noelle looked pensive. "No, not really. Mama would sometimes take me for tea when we were in Town. Nurse scrubbed my face so hard it hurt, then I would have to sit very still, very straight, and only Aunt Sylvia would talk. It was just like church. Once she put a plate of bonbons near me and said I might have one. There were sugar mice and glacé violets and chocolate-dipped strawberries—I couldn't choose! And she shouted at me that I wasn't picking a winner at Ascot, where was my sense of decision? Well, I was only seven or eight and I said I could decide quite well, thank you, I wished them all. Mama was mortified, of course, but Aunt Sylvia only laughed and had a servant tic up all the candies in a napkin for me to take home. We all had some.

"I remember that she had a huge red wig. She said it was the Wycombe auburn hair, just like mine and Mama's, only hers kept slipping. I worried and worried that my hair would fall sideways, until Nurse told me it was a wig."

"I don't recall her at all, Nellie. Why is that?" Ferne wanted to know.

"I suppose you were too young then, pet, and after Papa died we had to give up the London house and move to Derbyshire permanently. Great-aunt Sylvia never visited us here at Sterlingwood; she and Mama were quite estranged by then. It had something to do with Papa's funeral. We never travelled to London any more either, there was so much to do and so little money. Then Mama took sick, and Great-aunt Sylvia was travelling. I only heard from her once, when Mama died, just a short note really. I always wondered what finally came between them. . . ."

Two things had come between the autocratic, spinsterish Lady Sylvia Wycombe and the niece she had raised. One was Winston Armstrong, fifth Viscount Sterling of that line, and father of the present Viscount, lovingly called Winnie by his family. The other pull in the fabric of their relationship was Lady Wycombe's inability to refrain from saying "I told you so." She said "I told you so" when Armstrong died, leaving his widow nearly impoverished, with three young children, an encumbered estate and a great many debts. She had previously called the Viscount a penniless rake, which he was, an irresponsible wantwit here-and-thereian, which he was not, and destined to make her niece's life miserable, which he did only by leaving it. The Viscount had indeed earned for himself a

9

colourful reputation in his salad days, wending through his patrimony and each Season's debutantes with equal élan, and yet his raffish, boyish charm always shone through . . . for the younger Miss Wycombe at any rate. He had the fair, cherubic looks inherited by his two youngest children, guinea-gold curls and blue eyes, and Miss Felice Wycombe *would* have him, with or without her aunt's blessings.

Their first child, born on Christmas Day following a fairy-tale honeymoon in Paris, was named Noelle. The infant was purposely and with high principles *not* called Sylvia, although she did have the Wycombe colouring and although Lady Wycombe was the wealthiest member of either family. In a sudden stroke of parental accountability, the Viscount took a position with the Foreign Office, where he was an immediate success, for who makes a better ambassador than a reformed womanizer? All practiced charm and passing sincerity, he was always ready to travel anywhere, to smooth whatever ripples formed on diplomatic waters. Sent on missions by the King himself, the Viscount had all the trappings of a consul, without, however, the empire's exchequer. Unfortunately, his brand of diplomacy centered on lavish dinners, elegant turnouts and, rumour had it, bedchamber negotiations. As Aunt Sylvia was fond of repeating, he was an expensive bit of goods.

His wife did not have the strength for that type of life, nor the temperament. She much preferred staying at home, tending her babies and her roses. His country summoned the Ambassador, as he liked to be called, and he went. She stayed, and Aunt Sylvia said "I told you so." Yet his lady's love never diminished nor, to judge by his letters, extravagant gifts and visits as often as possible, did the Viscount's love for his wife. His fidelity may have been in question; his devotion, never. Who else would have travelled across the Continent with two young puppies in his greatcoat pockets, just because they were of a breed that was new to him? The tiny, long-haired white dogs were called Maltese, but the Viscount first saw them in Italy, not on the Island of Malta. He was told that the Greeks and the Romans had been fond of the breed, and he knew instantly that his wife, Felice, would rather this gift than another frippery jewel or whatever. As usual, he knew what would please a woman. (Hence the current basketful of snowy puppies by the hearth, plus numerous other Maltese dogs about.) Please her he might, and love her he most certainly did, yet he did not manage to provide well for his loyal Felice. His death some six years previously had left his family in sore straits indeed. The entailed property at Sterling showed every evidence of an absentee landlord; his debts were found to be mountainous, the family coffers empty.

It was at this point, the Viscount's funeral, that Aunt Sylvia issued her last self-satisfied smirk. Her generous offer to take the bereft family in was accompanied by a great many disparaging remarks about loose fish, fribbles and rakeshames. Of the dead speak nothing but good, *nihil nisi bonum*, etc., especially to the dead one's loving widow, who in this instance, from the depths of her sweet and peace-loving soul, dredged forth some of that awesome Wycombe pride. The London house was sold to pay debts. The widow's portion and her jewels went for rebuilding tenants' houses and restocking herds. Winnie's education money drained farmland and instead of Latin and Greek, the fourteen-year-old lad learned lambs and goats. Noelle at sixteen willingly sacrificed her small dowry to repair the roof over their heads. She mastered the art of baking bread when she should have been breaking hearts. The family retrenched, and Aunt Sylvia was consigned to the devil, whose hand she was most probably just now shaking.

Lady Sterling survived her husband by four years. They were hard years, especially for one who had been born to Town life and every convenience, but there were no complaints. Sighs, yes, to see Noelle actually tending the kitchen garden—and getting freckles!—and little Ferne picking strawberries like a barefoot wood nymph instead of walking in the park with her nanny. Young Winnie, educated to the best of the local vicar's ability, would be fine. He took to the land like a yeoman farmer, with his father's sheer joy of life itself. Knowing Sterlingwood was his gave the boy an outlet for his boundless energy. No, the widow's regrets were not for the new viscount but for her daughters. Where could they make their come-outs or meet eligible gentlemen? Certainly not in the farmlands of Derbyshire, so how could they make good marriages? Her one impossible hope, as she darned and redarned the sheets, was to give her girls their debutante Seasons in London. Two years after her death, the dream was going to come true. Aunt Sylvia had finally run out of I told you so's.

"And about time, too," Hattie said cryptically, ending with a hiccough after refilling and downing her glass for the third time. Noelle moved the decanter to another table, giving her aunt a fond hug in passing. Hattie began to sniffle, searching in the workbasket for a handkerchief this time. It was this aunt, the late viscount's sister Harriet Deighton, widow of an army officer, who immediately offered the motherless children a home, albeit only furnished rooms in Bath. But instead she had moved to Derbyshire, giving up her genteel poverty and friends of similar age and circumstances for a house brimful of young people and puppies. She had no head for figures and no experience of management, leaving Noelle to struggle alone, yet there was always something to be mended, collars to be turned or long curls to be braided.

"I . . . I have been so happy with you, dears, happier than I have been since before the dear Colonel was taken, and I am so pleased at your good fortune. And . . . and I want you to know I shall take care of everything here for you while you are in London and I—"

"Aunt Hat," Noelle declared, "no such thing! Where did you ever get such a hubble-bubble notion?" (If Noelle privately believed the sad idea came from the sherry decanter, she tactfully would not mention it.) "You are absolutely crucial to the venture; we must have a chaperone, of course. Did you think we would hire some down-at-the-heels old peeress to bear-lead us around and call us bumpkins for all that? Gammon!"

"But, Noelle, I have no high connections, you know."

"She's right, Nell," Winnie put in. "I know you'll want to make a splash, but how do you intend to do it when we don't know a soul in London?"

"Well, we will just have to make sure we meet them, the right people, that is. This is going to take some planning, of course. We don't have a great deal of time—the Season is so short and just a few months away—and I know you won't want to leave the Strubbings to run things here for too long, Winnie.

We don't have a great deal of money either, the solicitor says, with most of the income going just to keep the town house. So we will need to work out a strategy." Noelle raised her pointed chin and started pacing the worn green carpet of the small drawing room.

"Aye-aye, Captain." Winston laughed, well used to his elder sister's taking command of the situation. "Where do we start?"

"With a list, of course. Ferne, you get the paper and the pencil."

"Oh Nellie, not another of your lists!" her sister complained. "You are forever writing things down, and you know that half the times you lose the list itself!"

They all laughed, including Noelle, who admitted *some* occasional lapses from her good organizational ability. But this time she was serious. London's Society, the *ton*, did not simply accept strangers into its hallowed ranks, nor were breeding and money in themselves passports. Noelle knew this from her childhood days, from her mother's tales and from such glimpses of the London *Gazette* that infrequently came her way. Without that nod from the hostesses, she knew, without that acknowledgement by the leaders of the Beau Monde that yes, the Armstrongs did indeed meet up to the standards, they would be outcasts. No balls or Venetian breakfasts, no invitations for house parties, no clubs on St. James's for Win, no cozy teas with ladies of her own age for Aunt Hattie. They may as well stay in Derbyshire for the spring lambing. But no, Noelle Armstrong was not going to let Society snub its nose at *her* family. That Wycombe auburn hair went with a firm backbone. Her voice took on an unfamiliar determination; her pacing grew quicker. One of the dogs decided the sofa was a safer place after all, making a flurried dash of white feather duster to get to it.

"Before we can make a plan, we have to know our strengths and weaknesses," Noelle began. "We are already aware that we are unacquainted with anyone, thoroughly green and somewhat limited in financial resources, so let us not belabour that point." If she heard Win's chuckle, she ignored it. "But our strengths, hmm. Ferne, are you ready?" At her sister's smiling nod, pencil poised, Miss Noelle Armstrong, age twenty-two, heiress, began her campaign.

"Assets. First, Great-aunt Sylvia's town house. I recall it being modest, on the outskirts of Mayfair, which should still be quite fashionable. Next, we have a genuinely respectable chaperone."

"Noelle, dear, I have been thinking," Hattie interrupted. "Some of my friends in Bath have relatives in London. Perhaps if I wrote some letters we might gain an introduction or two. Do you think so?"

"Marvelous, Aunt Hattie. I knew we couldn't get along without you," Noelle replied. "And do you know who else I thought of? Who would know London inside and out and tell us just how to go on? Taylor!"

"Papa's valet?" Ferne was dubious, but Win let out an enthusiastic whistle.

"Of course! He wasn't just a valet, Ferne, he was almost an aide, butler, secretary, even coachman and cook sometimes. Papa used to say Taylor knew more state secrets than Mr. Pitt."

Noelle took it up: "And he knew all the *on dit*'s and all the styles and all the butlers in every fashionable household. Mama believed that more reputations were made or lost at The Duck and the Drake where Taylor relaxed than at Almack's or White's. Think of how he could help us, with servants and entertaining and just knowing who was who! Do you think he will come, Win?"

"Well, he is living with a sister in Sussex, I think. After a life with the Ambassador, he is either finally catching up on his sleep or itchy with boredom. He was used to being one of the family; I'll bet he'll come."

"Put him down as an asset, Ferne, but put a question mark. I shall write to him tomorrow. What's next?"

When no one answered Noelle continued her thoughtful pacing until a mewing sound from the basket near the hearth caught her attention. She stopped there and, kneeling, petted the mother dog and gently stroked the nursing puppies. When she straightened up she was smiling.

"What a bunch of geese we are! We want to bring ourselves to the *ton*'s notice, in a proper manner certainly, and we are overlooking two of our best attractions: Ferne's beauty and Win's title!'' Ferne gasped, but Noelle went on in her usual straightforward manner. "Don't go getting missish on me, Ferne. You know you're the prettiest girl hereabouts and there is no saying but you'd be a regular diamond in London, what with proper dressing and all. No more hiding your light under a bushel! Every man will want to meet you and, Win, stop sputtering. The mother of every hopeful debutante will want you at her parties, an attractive gentleman of property, and a Viscount to boot. You'll be irresistible! And no one can have you at their parties without having us, so there!''

"Cut line, Nell. That horse won't run,'' Win declared. "I have no desire to get leg-shackled.'' The young man ran his finger around his collar as though the very idea were a noose.

"And, Nell, you're making it sound like some dreadful auction where we'll be paraded on exhibit and sold to the highest bidder,'' Ferne cried.

It was no such thing, as Noelle explained, even if the London Season was also known as the marriage market. Neither of her siblings would ever be forced into a marriage of convenience, not when the family fortunes were so low, certainly not now when the tide was rising. No grasping mama was going to latch on to Winnie's title as a trophy for her whey-faced chit either, and no man would *ever* win Ferne's hand unless his heart—and hers—was firmly committed. There would be no loveless unions in this family, Noelle announced in the best manner of one of Mrs. Radcliffe's heroines. But where except in London was Ferne to meet this paragon, this noble, handsome gentleman, well-to-pass, it was hoped, who would cherish her as she deserved, not just admire her looks?

For certain he was not in the vicinity, for all the spotted, stammering, blushing lads had already been languishing after Ferne for years, with no more encouragement than a shy smile, eyes modestly cast down. So yes, if men were attracted to Ferne's loveliness, Noelle stated proudly, with no hint of jealousy, then all the easier to find the one Ferne could love. In the meantime a little Town bronze or polish would not be amiss, especially for Winston, before he settled into the Derbyshire soil like some oak tree putting down roots. After all, an asset was anything of value, and heaven knew they had little enough of that.

The entire family was laughing by now to see Noelle on one of her crusades, arms waving, cheeks flushed with resolution, reddish brown curls tumbling out of their ribbon to frame her face in an enchantingly dishevelled manner.

"And what will you bring to the bold venture, oh fearless leader," Win asked in his joking way, "besides a desire to pitchfork us into the middle of the *ton?* I know, we shall be Beauty"—with a nod to Ferne—"Rustic Beast; in this case, of course, Lord Rustic Beast"—a courtly bow—"and the Heiress, all overcoming men's, and women's, baser motives."

"No, you gudgeon, there is not enough money in Aunt Sylvia's estate to tempt anyone. And if you think that fact won't be known in Town as soon as we arrive, you do not know London ways. Puffing it up will only give people a distaste for us. No, if this is all to be like some wondrous fairy tale, which it is, you know, then I shall guard our finances, try to keep us out of scrapes and wait to announce that we shall all live happily ever after."

"That's our Nell, the brains of the family," Win teased. "Maybe we can find some nabob for you anyway, one who ain't too particular about freckles!"

"Wretch! Why don't you and Ferne ride over to Squire's to tell Sally our good news? We are going to need Squire Turner's help too, to advise Strubbing while we are gone and keep an eye out for us. And, Ferne, ask Sally and her mother if they have a current issue of *La Belle Assemblée* we could borrow."

"Do put on your lined boots, dear," Aunt Hattie reminded Ferne, who put down her paper and pencil and knelt at the basket near the hearth before leaving. She spoke softly to the mother dog, telling her to stay, to take care of her babies, then she picked up one pink-and-white wiggling little mass. She nestled it by her cheek, turning to her sister.

"You know, Nellie, we forgot another of the Armstrongs' assets. We have the puppies!"

After the two youngest Armstrongs left, Aunt Hattie resumed her knitting and Noelle sat by her, absently rubbing the silky ears of the dog at her side, a smile on her face. Her aunt's voice finally disturbed her reverie.

"Will I what, Aunt Hattie? I'm sorry, I wasn't attending."

"I said, *will* you be content merely to direct your happy farce? Have you no ambitions of your own?"

"If you mean will I search for a man to marry, I don't know. I never thought about it."

Indeed she never had. There was simply no one in the neighbourhood for her to consider, and no opportunity to travel farther. At twenty-two she did not exactly consider herself on the shelf, never having been off it, so to speak. Marriage had just not been on her list of possible futures. In fact, Noelle had only recently begun to consider her own future as separate from that of her family and Sterlingwood. She had been a part of it all for so long, a necessary, loving, working partner, but now they were all growing up. Noelle had already decided to seek a position as governess or housekeeper somewhere, when Winnie brought home a bride. Sterlingwood was not big enough to house two mistresses, and Noelle was too accustomed to doing things her own way. Ferne would marry, of course; she was too lovely for anything else. If a farmer's son it had to be, Ferne would be content; she had hardly known any other life. Noelle ached to think of it, her elfin sister wed to some uncultured clod, but give Ferne her dogs and horses and lambs—and yes, someone to care for her—she would be satisfied. Not Noelle. So used to being around Ferne's beauty, the smooth gold ringlets, the huge, innocent blue eyes, the creamy skin with its soft blush, Noelle never regarded her own looks as pleasing. With her own unruly, wispy auburn curls, green eyes that seemed to see everything, alabaster skin she only labelled insipid and freckles—of all the worst fates!—Noelle did not consider herself attractive to the boys who flocked around Ferne. Quite honestly, she had never cared. The young ones seemed like unlicked cubs, and what few older bachelors or widowers there were only bored her. Miss Noelle Armstrong would rather sleep alone than share her bed with a man whose only conversation was about crops and feeds. She liked them well enough—Nellie was not a snob—but she remembered her father, how gay he was, how elegant. He had always seemed very wise to her, even if he did not know the difference between a shoat and a sow! And she remembered how much her parents had loved each other. If Noelle could not have *that*, she had decided, she would seek employment.

That future had always been, well, in the future to her. Winnie was not at all anxious to wed, although Squire was looking at him like a prospective son-in-law, and Sally would make him a good, comfortable wife if they decided to make a match of it. And Ferne was only seventeen. But suddenly everything was changed. The future was *now*. They were set to go to London, to scrape together what monies they could for one glorious Season. At the least, they should all see something besides trees and cows! At the best, there would be no trouble firing Ferne off, with just the proper introductions. And if Winnie met a girl, preferably well dowered, all to the good. Then Noelle could see about a life of her own, not having to worry about the others. There was a house, there was some money, anything could happen. . . . They were going to London!

=== 2 ===

AUNT SYLVIA'S TOWN HOUSE

THE LONDON SEASON officially commenced each April with the first performance of the Opera. Many of the *ton* trickled back to Town some weeks earlier, to open their houses, refurbish their wardrobes and in general make ready for three arduous months of enjoying themselves. Miss Armstrong plotted her grand campaign to allow one month in Derbyshire while the advance guard, Taylor, scouted the terrain, and a full month in London for reconnoitering and outfitting the troops before entering the fray.

The first month passed in a hailstorm of lists and letters, to Bath, to the London solicitor, to Taylor in Sussex. The latter, retired to his sister's cottage on the coast, had to give long, serious deliberation to Miss Armstrong's request. He was packing his bags before the postboy was halfway down the street; he reached London before his letter of acceptance reached the Armstrongs in Derbyshire. Taylor, inestimable man, took upon himself the tasks of hiring staff, provisioning the house and paving the way. If some of the younger grooms and parlourmaids looked enough like Taylor to be nieces and nephews, at least, and if the new cook was a buxom, hearty lass, and if some of the new bottles in the wine cellar had never seen a custom's stamp, well, Taylor had not wasted all of his time on the Sussex coast. Wasn't he the Ambassador's man, and honour-bound to do right by the last Viscount's family? Such did he relate to his cronies at The Duck and the Drake, while picking up the meagre crop of out-of-season backstairs gossip and casting a few seeds of his own for future harvest. Anyone curious about the pedigree of the handsome young family soon to take up residency at No. 4 Chauncey Square would only have to consult his butler or valet. Taylor had his professional pride, after all.

The family, meanwhile, were making ready for their departure, locating Holland covers or dust sheets for the furniture, deciding what necessities had to travel with them in the coach (Aunt Hattie's hartshorn) and which could be shipped ahead by post (calves' foot jelly). The lumbering old travelling carriage had to be dragged from the stables, repaired and repainted; Sam, a farmhand, was fitted with livery to drive it. As Strubbing said, Sam had not done a lick of work since old man Gallagher's Peggoty went into service in London, so he could easily enough be spared. It took a full week to convince a tearful Ferne that some of the dogs had to remain behind, that they would be much happier in their own baskets in Mrs. Strubbing's kitchen. She was only satisfied when her bosom-bow Sally promised to look in on them and write faithfully. Only the puppies were to make the journey with the parent dogs: Jasmine, the mother and Ferne's own particular favourite, and Plato, the sire, who had adopted Noelle at his weaning and had hardly left her side since.

It might be expected that the ladies would go into a positive orgy of purchasing new clothes, perhaps travelling as far as Chesterfield for the latest fashions. But no, they each had one good woolen travelling outfit done up, along with one or two walking dresses as au courant as the local seamstresses could manage, studying the fashion plates of the *Ladies' Journal*. That way, the Armstrongs felt, they would be well enough dressed to face the London modistes. Anyone who cannot understand a female's buying a new outfit in which to shop for a new wardrobe, well, he will never understand women.

Winston was busy conferring with Squire and Strubbing about the property, walking nearly every inch of the land. Strubbing, elevated to the title of estate manager, nodded his head and made note of Winnie's instructions. Since Strubbing had been born to a tenant farmer right there and had taught the young Viscount all Win now knew about farming, it was expected that Sterlingwood would survive, if not prosper, during its master's absence.

High hopes and high spirits went hand in hand, but neither

was riding in the carriage when the Armstrongs finally began their journey. Aunt Hattie, in a dither, was checking all the bags, boxes and parcels stowed around her. Was there enough food in the hampers? Did she have enough wool for the scarf she was knitting? Where was her vinaigrette? Ferne was all red-eyed and splotchy from the past hour of farewells—not even *her* beauty could withstand such a bout of crying—and sat in a corner, weeping into a lacy scrap of cambric. Winston rode alongside the coach, a pistol tucked in his waistband, feeling very much the hero protecting his womenfolk, thinking what a lark it was. This lasted all of half an hour, till he was thoroughly bored and damp from the early mist. He hitched his horse to the back of the carriage and climbed up beside Sam Coachman, pulled his beaver hat over his eyes and proceeded to nap. And Noelle? There was the heiress, her hair already tumbling out of its knot from her last-minute exertions, the wisps near her face curling up from the dampness. She felt messy and tired. After all those weeks of details, the last days of packing and carrying and tidying up, the entire house at sixes and sevens, had come the last hours of repacking to find Aunt Hattie's spectacles. Noelle was irritable, too. Half was due to Ferne's sniffling, when the girl was headed for the happiest adventure of her life; the other half of Noelle's ill humour was due to the fact that after all her planning and consideration for every detail of her family's comfort and security, the warmed bricks and stuffed hampers, she, Noelle, got stuck riding backwards, with a lapful of puppies!

The journey was slow. Between job horses, winter-rutted roads, Noelle's occasional queasiness and frequent stops to air—for want of a better word—the puppies, it seemed endless. The inns along the way were generally cold and damp, with lumpy beds—who had slept there last?—and indifferent food. Noelle decided she would take in boarders at Aunt Sylvia's town house if she had to, rather than make the return journey.

Then, finally, they were at the house. By comparison, the carriage ride did not seem so bad anymore.

Chauncey Square was lovely, a remote cul-de-sac with rows of neat grey stone houses facing a tiny patch of green, away from all the hubble-bubble of the London traffic. With its brass gates, No. 4 was as sedate and proper as the others, one would have thought, the perfect home for an unwed aunt, until one saw the inside! There was Taylor, dignified and elegant, his waistline gaining what his hairline was losing, but as straight as ever and so familiar and welcoming among . . . among *things* made out of elephants' feet; sofas designed to resemble crocodiles, with claws; sarcophagi standing in the halls or set down as end tables to hold unidentifiable knickknacks; and stuffed beasts all over, with recriminating eyes.

Aunt Hattie's mouth hung open. Even Winnie, for once, was dumbfounded. It was too much for Noelle. Where was all the delicate Sheraton furniture she remembered, the portraits of the ancient Wycombe ancestors, the heirloom tapestries?

"I . . . I think I would like to see the bedrooms, Taylor, if you please."

"Surely, Miss Noelle. I have put you in Lady Wycombe's chamber, with your permission. It is on the right at the head of the landing."

Perhaps no one wanted to remain below with the dead creatures—what was in a sarcophagus anyway?—but they all trooped into Great-aunt Sylvia's bedroom as Taylor stood aside, his face expressionless in the finest butler tradition. Aunt Hattie gasped, Ferne blushed, Win let out one long whistle, while Noelle gave in and went off into whoops. A huge bed, all draped in red satin, occupied most of the room, with its canopy held by four naked houris. There was a shaggy fur throw on the floor, undressed nymphs and satyrs chasing one another across the clothes press, and mirrors everywhere.

"Why Aunt Sylvia, you gay old dog!"

Happily it was discovered that besides her fine taste in heiresses, Aunt Sylvia had yet another redeeming quality: She never threw anything away. The first order of business was an exploration of the attics, reclaiming the graceful old furnishings Noelle remembered, including a few Chippendale pieces, and exchanging them for the oddities of Sylvia's travels and the current fad for things Egyptian. Armstrongs and footmen met on the stairwells to trade a Claude Lorrain landscape for a collection of dead beetles under glass, chintz-covered chairs for a straw basket-thing with cushions that had been suspended from a chain in the drawing room. A fine collection of Orientalia was delegated to the morning room, which instantly became the Chinese room. Some of the items Noelle felt must be of value, to someone; some of the old furniture needed recovering. What a pleasure it was to hear Taylor say "I shall have the appraiser in," or "Mr. Kesstler will bring swatches tomorrow." How provident to have enough strong footmen to move the heavy pieces around until everything was just the way Noelle liked it. A magnificent Turkey carpet was unearthed for her bedroom, new hangings ordered, Gainsborough's portrait of a much younger Aunt Sylvia hung where unabashed cupids had played. The others' bedrooms were quite ordinary English chambers, and the library was found to be a comfortable place for the family to gather until the more formal rooms were restored. Her house in order, or nearly so, it was time to get to more serious concerns—clothes.

Madame Franchot was the premiere modiste of the day. To be seen in her creations meant that you knew what was best, and could afford it. Since Madame could not possibly outfit every woman with money and high aspirations, her clientele grew more and more select. Madame Franchot herself chose the ladies to be so graced; Noelle could not hope to be one of them, even if the Armstrong finances could be stretched so far. Yet there were ways, ways that included Noelle's butler, Madame's pretty young apprentice and some bolts of smuggled French silk. This last arrived from Sussex, wrapped in oilskins, under a cartload of potatoes. The less said about the transaction the better, except that Madame Franchot was delighted to create a few special gowns for the ladies.

"I do not think Papa would have approved of this, Taylor," Noelle fretted.

"But miss, you recall how the Ambassador always enjoyed good wine, and how he always liked his ladies to be dressed fine and smell pretty—"

"You mean there are perfumes, too? We'll end in Newgate!"

For the bulk of their wardrobe Madame Franchot herself

recommended one of the newer establishments. Called *Les Cousines*, this partnership was eager for new business and therefore promised to be reasonable, quick and as fashionable as Mademoiselle Armstrong desired. Despite the recommendation, Noelle hesitated; this was a crucial decision. Princess Charlotte could dress any which way, look a quiz or a dowd. Miss Nobody from Upper Puddlejump had better dress quite up to the mark if she did not want to be cast as a milkmaid. While Noelle was deliberating, one of the cousins, if indeed the three women were related at all, was showing the ladies some gowns already completed. The first one was a jonquil muslin walking dress with tiny blue flowers embroidered on the sleeves and the bodice and ribbons of the same colour falling from under the high waist down to the hem. Ferne turned beseechingly to her sister, those big blue eyes shining—the almost identical forget-me-not blue of the ribbons—and there was no question. The dress was perfect. Aunt Hattie declared that she knew as much about fashion as she did about steam engines, but she could recognize quality when she saw it, so the ladies were committed. Noelle was even more firmly convinced to patronize this shop when the eldest dressmaker showed such sense and understanding:

"You wish to—how do you say?—cut a dash, no? But it must be everything that is proper, I think. For the *jeunesse* it must be white and the pastels, of course, very pure, showing off the innocence, the fragility. Everything *petite* and very delicate, like dressing a doll. Bah, she would look beautiful in a flour sack! There is no challenge." The modiste dismissed Ferne with a snap of her fingers, then proceeded to walk around Noelle, studying her more generous proportions, touching one of the russet curls, undone as usual and trailing down her back, turning Noelle's face to the window light.

"Yes, elegant, *ravissante*. We shall use colours and textures and lines of the most classic. Mademoiselle has the figure, nothing to hide. A woman of sophistication, of . . . of—*qu'est-ce que c'est?*—desirability, without a hint of availability."

Noelle was thrilled at this new picture of herself. Could she really look like a woman of experience, she who had never kissed a man? She was more than willing to stand still while her measurements were taken, weaving air castles around this new person she was to become. Madame Celeste's parting advice brought her back to earth:

"You must always use the parasol. Perhaps the *tache de son,* those . . . those freckles . . . can be covered with powder, *n'est-ce pas?*"

There were fabrics and colours and styles to choose, and did they really need so many dresses, Ferne asked, concerned at such extravagance.

"Don't worry, pet, we are doing quite well, and we can always sell some of Aunt Sylvia's jewelry—or one of her mummies!" Or, Noelle thought to herself, Taylor's sister might be sending him another load of "potatoes."

When the ladies were all satisfied, even Aunt Hattie being convinced that she must do them proud, in new gowns of mauve and lavender-blue and a charming grey to offset her hair, they moved on. Dresses, even morning dresses, riding habits, ball gowns, dresses for teas, for carriage rides, for walking, for dining, were not enough. There were still laces and trims to purchase, shoes and gloves, fans and stockings, beaded reticules and cashmere shawls, the entire Pantheon Bazaar, in fact, or so it seemed. Luckily Taylor's foresight had sent an extra footman along with their new abigail, Moira, just to carry packages. For three women who had been used to doing for themselves and one another, one ladies' maid was ample, Noelle had insisted. Taylor's niece Moira suited them all, where a London dresser would only have intimidated them. The new abigail was polite, and also friendly, chatty and eager to please. She walked the proper two steps behind her mistresses, yet enjoyed herself as much as they did, especially at the milliners' shops. If there were thirty in the Bond Street vicinity, the Armstrong ladies must have visited them all. Aunt Hattie had a stock of lace caps, but her nieces had always owned two bonnets each, one for everyday wear, one for special occasions. A new ribbon had been a treat. Let it suffice that more than one London bonnet-maker allowed herself an extra strawberry tart with afternoon tea that week. Moira was the delighted recipient of four used bonnets. A new feather though, or maybe a cluster of fake cherries, and chance was she would catch the eye of that handsome coachman from the country.

While the ladies were thus employed, Winston was also undergoing a change, from casual country gentleman to Town buck. Taylor himself escorted the young Viscount to Stultz, Scott and Weston, Brummell's own tailor, for his coats, Hoby for his boots, until Winston, too, was complete to a shade. Nothing of the dandy about him, he insisted, but a fellow wanted to look all the crack if he was going to have two beauties on his arms! He even visited Petersham's favourite snuff shop, then stood before a mirror for hours, practising how to open the snuff box with one hand, as the Prince's friends did. He and Sam Coachman also spent a great many hours looking in at Tattersall's and the other horse auctions. Sam, who had an eye for horses, besides an eye out for his Polly, directed Winston to a team of chestnuts, high-bred but well mannered, perfect for the ladies and Aunt Sylvia's town chaise. It did not take much urging for Noelle to convince Win to purchase at her expense his, and every young man's, dream: a shiny black curricle, the wheels picked out in gold, and a glossy pair of spirited blacks.

"Sweetest goers you've ever seen, Nellie, best of good sisters! I am taking them out to Richmond in the morning to get the feel of it, you know, before taking them to Hyde Park." He gave her an affectionate hug. "Truly, Nell. I'm more grateful than I can say. I am yours to command."

"Good." Noelle smiled. "The dancing master arrives at three o'clock. Be here."

"Dancing lessons" —squawk—"I say, Sis—"

"Don't be a gapeseed," Ferne admonished. "Of course you must have lessons, too. What if we should be invited to a ball and we don't know anyone present? Think of how it would look if no one asked us to dance." She ignored Win's muttered "Hardly likely," and went on: "We would have to sit with the chaperones and wallflowers. People would think we were antidotes! But if our brother is there to partner us, we will seem popular so everyone will want to stand up with us."

Win was looking confused. Before he could question Ferne's

peculiar variety of logic, Aunt Hattie reminded him that he would have other obligations.

"When you accept an invitation you are expected to dance, even with some of the antidotes and ape leaders. Someone has to, and you would not want to step on the poor girls' feet besides, would you? Your father was considered one of the best dancers of his day and even Colonel Deighton, dear soul, was very graceful."

When the lessons commenced and the Armstrongs were introduced to the waltz, Winston allowed as how this was not half bad. "I would not mind holding some dainty handful so close, I guess." He held up his hands, exclaiming, "No, I ain't in the petticoat line! Just practising for my duty dances, don't you know."

After the dancing master came the hairdresser, Monsieur Françoise himself. Monsieur spoke rapidly in French, to no one in particular, as he pulled the pins from Ferne's hair, letting it fall like a golden shower down her back. A gather, a twist, a snap of his fingers to the watchful abigail for pins, another snap for the curling iron, a moment when Noelle was afraid to speak—*et voila!* Perfection. Ferne's hair was like a crown, smoothly twined atop her head, with one long, perfect curl gracing her left shoulder. The maid exhaled loudly.

Monsieur began on Noelle, the same unintelligible muttering, the pins falling, the lifting and releasing of individual curls to test their habits. "No, no. It is all wrong."

"M'sieur?" asked Moira, afraid she was being blamed by the great Françoise, and after only five days of service to her ladies.

Without answering, the hairdresser removed a pair of scissors from his pocket, a tiny little scissors such as might be used for embroidery, and began cutting. It was a painstaking operation, nearly a life's growth of hair falling to the floor curl by curl like russet autumn leaves around Noelle, who had her eyes scrunched up tight after the first snip. Again Monsieur's peremptory snap of the fingers, and Noelle felt the curling iron, and again and again.

"Nellie, it's gorgeous!" Ferne gasped. "And all the rage!"

Indeed it was both, this style known as Grecian curls; only

27

the most courageous ladies dared to have their hair cropped so short. On Noelle it was perfect, a caplet of seemingly tousled curls framing her face. With a few ringlets on her forehead, the red-brown brushed with copper, her skin seemed even whiter, her green eyes even larger set under their dark lashes. The style looked neither *gamine* nor cherubic, only, as Monsieur himself declared, *"Très chic."* Did she hold her head higher? It was only because all that weight was gone, Noelle told herself.

Three young people and one widowed aunt newly arrived in London were not going to be satisfied with seeing only the insides of shops, stables and their own Chauncey Square house. There was so much else out there! Now, before the *ton* was back in Town, before the Armstrongs would be on display, trying to enter that most sophisticated of societies, they went sightseeing, like the provincials they were!

Westminster, St. Paul's, the Tower and the Crown Jewels. The Royal Exchange, where Ferne started to weep over the wretched conditions of the menagerie animals. Astley's Amphitheatre, where she felt she could teach her dogs some of the stunts the clowns had taught theirs. Noelle was thankful they were not back in the country, Win was so eager to try the trick riding.

There was even one memorable night at Vauxhall Gardens to eat paper-sliced ham and watch the fireworks. Vauxhall was out of fashion and, if Taylor was to be believed, it was positively dangerous if not decadent, with its Dark Walks and hidden pavilions, to say nothing of revelling cits. A fantastic spectacle with a hint of peril—what could be more delightful? Even if nothing else came from the Season, at least they would have had these pleasures, Noelle tried to convince herself. It was almost time for the campaign's first skirmish.

=== 3 ===

A LADY'S COMPANION

ON THE OPENING night of the Royal Opera no one cared what was to be performed or by whom. The audience itself was play enough; people went merely to see and to be seen. If, while being seen, one might be noted as having the largest diamond, the lowest décolletage, the highest shirtpoints or the most intricately tied cravat, all to the good. If all the world was a stage, and the operagoers players, they all wanted leading roles. Not so Ferne, who was embarrassed by all the attention the Armstrong box was attracting. There was a great deal of ogling from the gallery and lorgnette-raising from nearby boxes during the first act. During the intermission, however, one buck in the pit stood and, staring right up at Ferne, his hand over his heart, declared in a loud voice, "Oh Lord, I think I am in love." His cohorts all laughed, but Ferne was mortified. Bright pink, she tried to get Noelle to leave.

"No, we cannot go yet, and why should we? We have nothing to be ashamed of." Indeed they had not. Noelle lifted her straight little nose in haughty disdain for the boors in the cheap seats, but secretly she was so proud she could have burst her stays, if she had worn any. Ferne was a picture of classic English beauty in her pale-blue gown with white lace fichu, the single strand of her mother's pearls at her throat and a chain of pearls twined around the rich blond plaits gathered in a knot on her head. The blush even looked becoming with Ferne's creamy complexion. Ferne was the prettiest girl in the theatre, Noelle was sure. If the elder Miss Armstrong was receiving her share of the admiring scrutiny, she did not recognize it. Her family had complimented Noelle tonight, of course, and she felt very elegant in all her finery, but she was sublimely unaware of quite

29

how stunning she looked. Moira and she had decided on one of her plainest new gowns, a bottle-green silk with tiny puffed sleeves, simply gathered high under the bosom with gold braid, which was also used to scallop the hem. On her milky-white chest—of which more was showing than ever before—she wore a necklace from Aunt Sylvia's safe, a breastplate really, of some strange golden bird in flight. The bird's wingtips hung from a heavy gold chain, its feathers were inlaid with melted green glass and its single eye was a ruby. A gold fillet was threaded through Noelle's curls and across her brow in classic style. If she had heard the gossip she would have been disbelieving, then thrilled, that all of London would soon be talking of not one incognita, but two, an incomparable and an original.

Even Aunt Hattie looked dignified in her grey satin, with matching turban and white ostrich plume. No one was close enough to see that she was trying to read the program upside down, for want of her spectacles. It would not have upset her to be caught out either; not after the fortification Taylor had fetched her from the cellars, before this ordeal. Winston had done Taylor proud, in his black silk pantaloons and striped stockings, embroidered waistcoat, with only one fob, mind. His neckcloth had been tied by Taylor, not entrusted to the young valet he was training, in something called the Sterling Fall.

"It was how I used to tie the Ambassador's," Taylor related, a catch in his voice. It was no such thing, of course, the Ambassador always tying his own cravats, and ruining five or six in each attempt. Taylor was not going to go through *that* again. Winston looked truly elegant, and was truly afraid to move his head for fear of dislodging his curls, pomaded into the carefree *coup aŭ vent* style, or splitting a seam, so tight was his jacket. It had taken both Taylor and the new valet to ease it on.

"This is all a lot of hogwash anyway, Nellie. I feel like one of the beasts in the menagerie. I don't know why we had to come here to announce our appearance. Why couldn't we just have put a notice in the paper?"

Noelle had been daydreaming instead of listening to the Italian tenor. As her brother's words sank in, though, she turned to him in amazement, dropping her fan. "Winston, you are positively brilliant."

The Armstrongs left before the next intermission.

Two days later a notice did appear in the London *Gazette*, a boxed advertisement that read: "Finest companions now available to discriminating Ladies of Quality. Loyal, intelligent, clean white dogs of the Maltese breed. Inquiries No. 4 Chauncey Square. Five only, one hundred pounds each."

That afternoon, between the hours of four and five, when fashionable London was taking its constitutional, a carriage drove through the marble arches of Hyde Park. Its three occupants descended and began to walk along the pathways, chatting among themselves, nearly oblivious to the attention they were drawing, which was considerable. Anyone who had been to the Opera, or who had heard the gossip, recognized the two unknowns and the handsome Tulip who had to be a brother, so similar was he in looks and colouring to the younger beauty. The females were seen to be even more lovely up close, where one could note the startling clarity of Ferne's blue eyes, the coppery highlights of Noelle's curls as they peeped from under a very stylish chip-straw bonnet trimmed with violets. Both girls were dressed in the height of fashion again, Ferne in light blue, Noelle in dark, with white lace and ribbons, both carrying white muffs, even though the day was fairly warm. After walking a short distance from the carriage paths, each girl put down her muff, which sprouted four legs and a jaunty plumed tail curled over its back. The dogs, Jasmine and Plato, of course, followed right behind their mistresses, stopping when Ferne and Noelle paused to admire the shrubbery, sitting quietly by their feet when the girls sat on a bench for a moment before returning to the park entrance. There each girl picked up her muff. The Armstrongs departed.

The following morning the notice again appeared in the paper. The afternoon saw a slightly different scenario: A smart curricle entered the park, driven by the young blond gentleman, his adorable sister next to him, dressed in a carriage gown of the pink colour known as "maiden's blush." Her bonnet was trimmed with ribbon of the same colour, tied fetchingly to one side of her chin. On the narrow seat between the attractive couple sat one of the tiny white dogs, its forelock gathered in a matching pink ribbon so that black eyes and nose were visible. The dog stood and wagged its tail when another carriage approached, but only let out a short, sharp yip once, when a gentleman on a restive stallion rode close and tipped his beaver hat. With both hands on the reins, Win could only nod, while Ferne very properly looked down, telling the dog to shush. Again, a very charming picture, pretty behaviour to match.

The third day, another notice. This time the gentleman rode alongside while three women were driven in a chaise, the youngest and fairest with her back to the liveried driver. Two dogs by her side had their front feet on the carriage edge, their noses sniffing the breeze, long silky ears flying in the wind. The three ladies seemed very content with their own company. Passengers in nearby carriages could hear the young miss's soft chiming laughter and the older girl's richer chuckles, somehow in keeping with her more lively colouring. Even the older woman, a plump little matron with grey hair and a nearsighted squint, appeared to be smiling in a good-natured, affable manner. As before, the group circled the park once without recognizing anyone, then left.

"It's working, Nellie. Your scheme is working!" Winston congratulated his sister when the family was back in the library for tea. "Every man's eye was on your carriage—and every woman's eye was on her man, noticing it!"

"They were all staring, Nell. I felt so uncomfortable," Ferne complained. "Must we do this anymore?"

Noelle considered, twirling one of her new curls around a finger. "I do not think so, pet. We'll see what the advertisement brings, then we can probably be more approachable. Once we know some people it will not be such a fish bowl . . . and they certainly seemed interested in meeting us."

If Noelle's ambition was to make the *ton* curious, she had succeeded, beyond her dreams. Society was delighted to have something new to twitter about; a mystery was divine! Here was presented a handsome young man, a brother obviously, visibly and hopefully unattached; two exquisites properly chaperoned and well behaved—no lightskirts here; and money, as proved by the carriages, the gowns, the modality of it all. Who were these people?

And the dogs! No woman could miss the affecting pictures they made, matching ribbons and all, nor the admiration so evident in every gentleman. Why, when the strangers' coach went by, all conversations stopped as each escort's head swivelled. If having one of those little creatures could generate a similar degree of attention, every woman needed one. So what if one hundred pounds was an exorbitant fee, at least five times what the ordinary companion—two-legged variety—earned in a year? It was less than their husbands spent on a horse, and there were only five of the adorable beasties available, after all. They *must* be special, so anyone who owned one would, of course, be special. It was the principle of Madame Franchot again, where the Ladies of Quality wanted the first, the best, the most expensive, just because the other ladies wanted it.

Noelle's goal was not merely to liven up the city's social life, nor make bywords of the Armstrongs, à la Poodle Byng, who took his dogs everywhere with him. Nor was she primarily concerned with making such a profit on Jasmine's puppies. She had promised Ferne the pups would go to good homes only, and she meant it, and she was interested, as a true dog lover, in publicizing this breed her mother had loved. Her main goal, the one thing that meant her mother's ambitions and her own were fulfilled, however, could be expressed in one word: Almack's.

Almack's itself was nothing much, a mediocre sort of assembly hall. Being invited to attend the Wednesday night balls, though, was everything. Everything, that is, if you were desirous of becoming a member of High Society, of meeting the nobility on its own grounds, of finding an eligible *parti* for your sister! Men would always find a way to meet a girl as beautiful as Ferne, but the proper men? True gentlemen, with breeding, distinction, old family names—perhaps even money to support the ancestral ruins—were to be found at Almack's.

For a girl to get to Almack's she needed to have breeding, distinction, etc.—money did not hurt, although it could not have come from Trade—and an invitation from one of the patronesses. But one could not simply walk up to Sally Jersey or Princess Esterhazy, two of the high priestesses of Society's cult, and ask for a voucher. Nothing was less to the purpose than an encroaching display of poor manners. Besides, Noelle did not even *know* any of the patronesses. Before there could be an invitation, there had to be an introduction. This might come eventually, if the Armstrongs promenaded long enough in the public eye or some friend of their parents' took them up; or it might come by luck, if any of Aunt Hattie's secondhand Bath acquaintances moved in these higher circles and responded to the calling cards she was leaving; or it might happen by design. It was Noelle's plan to meet these Ladies of Quality on a perfectly genteel, refined level, explaining to them that the pups were already housebroken!

The plan was working . . . and not working. Many cards were being left, many footmen were being sent to No. 4 Chauncey Square to make inquiries. Taylor gathered them all for careful study. With his network of information, Taylor knew who had the most influence. Fully aware of Noelle's dilemma, he vowed he would retire for good if he couldn't get his ladies to Almack's. He gravely presented the Ambassador's daughter with a list of the most likely prospects.

"Lady Josephine Amberscott, Duchess of Ridge, Miss Noelle, is one of the *grande dames*. Not a patroness, but certainly with prestige. She is related to nearly every great family, giving many of them high expectations, so to speak, as the lady is childless, and one of the wealthiest women in London."

A footman was sent to see if it was convenient for Noelle and Ferne to call on Her Grace the following morning, but the messenger returned with the particularly well-endowed Duchess herself, so eager was the lady.

"I know it ain't proper," Lady Ridge said, over the hurriedly ordered tea in the Chinese room, "but at my age who gives a damn? Don't mean to put you to the blush, gel," she told Ferne. "In my day we were taught to speak our minds. Now who knows how much time I have left for roundaboutation? No, it's straight to the point, I always say. Knew your Aunt Wycombe, stiff-rumped old bag of wind. Knew your father too, handsome devil. The chit looks just like him. I met your mother once or twice, quiet kind of gel." She stared at Noelle, then told her, "You have your looks but you don't strike me as one of those niminy-piminy types."

"No, your Grace, I'm afraid not. I always thought speaking one's mind was perfectly proper, at certain times, of course."

"Putting me in my place, are you?" She cackled. "Can't blame you. Here I am, a fat old lady landing on your doorstep, checking out your family tree. Well, now what about those dogs?" She changed the topic abruptly. "That's why I took the liberty of coming by, you know, didn't want them all snapped up."

"Of course, your Grace," Noelle answered, recovering a bit. This was her first duchess, after all. She asked Ferne to fetch Plato and Jasmine.

"Plato, eh? What possessed you to name a little fellow like that?"

Noelle smiled. "Our father started it. He brought the original pair back from Italy for Mama. He was so impressed at how ancient the breed was. The Greeks knew them, possibly the Egyptians, too. My father was told that a Roman governor, Publius, had one named Issa in the year A.D. 25. There was even a poem about it written by the epigrammatist Martial." *

"Not important, gel, I want a dog, not a history lesson."

"Hmm. Yes, well, our father named the first two Socrates and Sappho. It had nothing to do with either's . . . er . . . tastes. After that Mama had Aristotle and Archimedes and Zeno, but she named the females after flowers. We had a Rose and a Violet, all white, of course, and Columbine is at home. Squire's wife has—but here are the parents of the new litter. I want you to see the adult dogs close up, so you will know what you are picking."

Lady Josephine lifted her lorgnette on its ribbon to survey the two dogs. Plato had gone straight to Noelle, then lain down, his chin resting on her shoe. Jasmine was cavorting around the tea

---

* "Issa is more frolicsome than Catulla's sparrow. Issa is purer than a dove's kiss. Issa is gentler than a maiden. Issa is more precious than Indian gems. . . . Lest the last days that she sees light should snatch her from him forever, Publius has had her picture painted."

tray, dancing on her hind legs until Ferne laughingly broke off a bit of pastry to feed her.

The Duchess said nothing, merely watching as she ate another biscuit. Noelle hesitated, trying to gauge the lady's interest. She drew an impression of coldness from the rounded face. Discouraged, Noelle still went on to expound the virtues of the breed, while Ferne had Jasmine roll over, sit up and shake hands, for morsels from the tea tray.

"As you can see," Noelle said quickly, afraid she was sounding like a school marm again and trying to get all of her facts across before the expected set-down, "these are very special dogs and must have special owners. They are healthy as a rule, but they do require daily grooming to look their best. We do not wish to see someone take a dog, then hand it over to the gardener, or mistreat it when she tires of it. These are *not* kitchen mongrels. In fact, we are so concerned with preserving the integrity of the breed and protecting our own dogs that we have a few conditions to present to each prospective owner." Noelle finished the last sentence on a note less firm than she had intended. When this was received with only a "Harumph," she continued nervously.

"No disrespect intended, your Grace, just that you promise to see the dog well cared for and if, at some time, you no longer want the animal, you will return it to us. This will be written on the bill of sale. Is that agreed?"

"Get on with it, gel. Do you think I am going to spend a hundred pounds and all this time on a mutt I'll show off twice and then give to my maid, like an old bonnet? I am not that kind of fool. No, I'm going travelling, off to visit a parcel of relatives spread all over the country, now that the weather is good, before it gets too hot. I'll miss the Season, but so what? I have seen enough milk-and-water misses to last a lifetime. And as for men, well, they just don't make them like they used to. No, I am going and I want a companion along the way. That's what you said in the *Gazette*, where I got the idea. And when I get to all those starched-up nincompoops I call relatives, the dog'll still be more entertaining than any of them! Better conversationalist, too, I'll bet a monkey on it. So let's see these precious mutts of yours!"

Noelle still had some reservations, until Ferne returned again, a puppy in each hand. She put them on the floor, where they proceeded to chase each other's tails, sniff the furniture and do battle with the carpet's fringe.

Lady Josephine remarked caustically, "Hand one here. If you put it on the floor I can't see it. I'm so fat I haven't seen my toes in years."

Ferne placed one of the pups in the Duchess's cupped palms. The dowager lifted the scrap for an eye-to-eye inspection—and a lick on the nose—then lowered it to the shelf formed by her ample bosom. The puppy, weighing two or three pounds at best, seemed content to be so cradled, especially with a pearl earring dangling so enticingly nearby.

The Duchess started cooing to it. Puppy love indeed!

"Your Grace, would you like to see another?" Ferne asked respectfully, ready to go fetch another pair.

"No, this little . . . girl, is it? . . . will do just fine. Delicious. In fact, I might just call her Crumpet. You can tell I've always been fonder of my food than of smelling the flowers. I can't wait to see my nevvies fawn all over the dog, trying to do me up sweet. Bunch of toadeaters, all of them. Serve 'em right if I leave Crumpet here all my money."

Ferne had already drawn up a sheet of the dog's genealogy ("The pup can count back more generations than most of the Ten Thousand. Wouldn't I love to serve *that* in Sally Jersey's teacup!" The Duchess chuckled.) and its diet, etc. Ferne was near to tears when Lady Josephine called for her carriage.

The Duchess patted her cheek and said kindly, "Never you fret, missy, I'll take good care of your pet. Just think of how happy it will make this fat old lady." As Ferne's blue eyes started to water she added, "You'll be too busy for this kind of companion anyway." On her way out she told Noelle, "You're good girls, both, but you have something between your ears besides a draft. I like to see that. But I already told the nodcocks I'm coming, so . . . If you're not hitched by the Fall Season, I'll take a hand in it. Got a lot of grand-nieces I wouldn't mind cutting out. You've got countenance, girl, you'll do."

"Lord and Lady Kingsley," Taylor intoned as he handed Noelle the next card, "are one of the first families. He is an advisor to the Prince. Lady Kingsley's elder daughter married a Marquis in her first Season. There is another daughter, Miss Ferne's age, who should be presented this year. The messenger implied that the dog was to be a gift for this young lady.''

Now if fortune were smiling, Miss Kingsley would have treasured her dog, made Ferne her bosom bow and introduced Ferne to other friends, whose parties she would then be invited to, etc.

Dame Fortune was apparently slightly indisposed. Miss Clarice Kingsley adored the puppy and agreed wholeheartedly to Noelle's stipulations for its well-being. She immediately named the dog after a heroine in one of Mrs. Radcliffe's novels, which she lent to Ferne, along with a collection of others. Miss Armstrong did in turn become a frequent visitor to Kingsley House on Portman Square, often bringing Jasmine so the dogs could visit while the girls chatted about books, dresses, daydreams. All of this took place, of course, in Miss Clarice Kingsley's bedchamber, where that lady sat on the bed, her broken leg in its heavy cast propped up on cushions. No presentation. No parties. No more jumping toll gates on green hunters.

Taylor's voice was almost shaking as he read the message written on the back of the card: " 'Sir Geoffrey Cox seeks the opportunity for his wife to select a companion dog.' Sir Geoffrey and Lady Cox are in the younger crowd. She was a reigning belle for two Seasons before her marriage. Now she is known for her style. She is dashing, elegant, highest *ton*.''

Lady Cox was everything Taylor had said, and more. About five months more. The dog was to be her compensation for missing the Season while she returned to Kent to await the blessed event.

"Now I won't be bored or lonely. I surely won't miss all the old tabbies at tea! And you say the breed is good with children?''

=== 4 ===

A YOUNG MAN'S FANCY

BESIDES HIS PRIDE, Taylor had six months' wages riding on his ladies getting to Almack's this Season. He was beginning to worry. Three dogs down, two to go. He was shuffling through the calling cards of the second echelon of interested buyers, those not so highly placed on the social scale, when just in the nick of time, and just in the best tradition of the Minerva Press, his heroines were saved. . . .

A card was sent from the Earl of Wrenthe, and you could hardly climb any higher on that same social scale, Taylor told himself, without bumping a royal arse. Relief made Taylor giddy, and possibly careless. He accepted the card from the footman without inquiring why, exactly, the Earl of Wrenthe, noted Corinthian, conscientious member of Parliament, advisor to the Home Secretary, man among men yet confirmed bachelor at age thirty-five (to the chagrin of one-half the eligible women in England, and one-third of the ineligible) should wish to purchase a lady's lapdog.

"Most likely for one of his sisters. There are two, I believe, both married," Taylor explained to Noelle. "There is also a married brother, with children, and another still at Oxford. It is said the Earl has no inclination to marry, with the succession so well assured."

"Maybe he is about to contract an engagement and wants the dog as a gift for his beloved," Ferne, ever the romantic, guessed.

"I do not believe it would go unremarked, if such a very sought-after gentleman was paying particular attention to any young lady," Taylor understated, "but it is possible."

"Well, we shall never know unless we see him," Noelle said practically. "And if he is everything you say, Taylor, wealthy, respected, intelligent and handsome, I for one cannot wait to meet the paragon."

Noelle was bound to be disappointed, for Justin Gerald Waverly Wrenthor, Earl of Wrenthe, was much too busy to undertake such a mission himself. There was the child labor bill coming up for debate, a conference on the flood damage to the properties in Cornwall, an appointment at Manton's Shooting Gallery that afternoon to test out some new pistols, two routs and a dinner that evening, besides a new folio of his friend Byron's poems just arrived. For a man with a reputation for not liking to exert himself, the Earl was extremely industrious. One of the advantages of being both wealthy and well placed, the Earl had learned at an early age, was that he never *had* to exert himself unless he wished it. It was too bothersome to worry about his clothes or his cattle, or whatever, so he only wore or drove the best, and hired the best men to care for them. It was much too tiresome to pay court to the silly chits thrown at his head, so he ignored them and their mamas. It was emotionally draining to be embroiled in duels, etc., so the Earl refused to be anything but the most amiable of good fellows, perfect manners notwithstanding. When you had established a reputation as a young man for being devilishly hot-at-hand, and extremely skillful with sword and pistols to boot, you could afford to be affable. No one dared rile you. If someone annoyed him now, the Earl just raised one expressively heavy eyebrow, or simply left. You could do that, if you were the Earl of Wrenthe. You could consider the issues of the world and human nature, and leave the humdrum, everyday errands (like sending your secretary to fetch a pet for your latest mistress) to others.

Noelle decided to be affronted that the Earl did not call in person. "If he is too stiff-necked to attend us himself, he cannot really be suitable. I mean, who would let someone pick out a *dog* for him?"

Taylor begged her to reconsider. "The Earl is known to be extremely civil, not high in the instep at all, pardon the expression. Perhaps he is just caught up in weightier matters."

"Yes, Noelle," Aunt Hattie put in, "the country is at war, you know. *Someone* must attend to that."

"Well, if you put it like that. At least we can speak to the secretary. Where did you put him, Taylor?"

"In the front drawing room, miss. He did give his name as James Waverly, so he must be a relation of the Earl's, a trusted relation, for such a position to so fine a gentleman."

"You've made your point, Taylor. Show Mr. Waverly in."

James Waverly was a pleasant-looking young man of about twenty-five who had no trouble charming all three ladies during tea, once he got over staring at Ferne. He admired Aunt Hattie's knitting, earned a great deal of Ferne's regard by showing his delight in Jasmine's antics, and Noelle's by his interest in the breed's history. He even asked Noelle to write the name of the author of the Cambridge tract, *Of Englishe Dogges,* so he could look up the medieval document sometime. It was with regret, Noelle explained, that she could not sell him a dog.

"We make it a policy, sir, to let our dogs go only when we know the new owners or at least the purchaser. That way we are assured that the dogs are truly wanted, not a surprise gift for a lady who actually admires cats. In addition, we like to know that the dog's personality matches its owner's. Do not laugh, Mr. Waverly. Each dog is different, the same as people."

"Noelle is right, Mr. Waverly, really." Ferne faced toward him, an angel beckoning to paradise; he almost forgot to breathe, much less listen. "Why, Lady Josephine wanted a dog to cuddle, while Clarice wants hers to romp after a ball. What if they got the wrong dog? They would be unhappy and the dogs would be, too. We could not have that, you do see, don't you, sir?"

All James Waverly saw were those big blue eyes. He nodded anyway, lost.

"Since you stated that you are not personally acquainted with the lady for whom Lord Wrenthe is purchasing the puppy, we must speak to the Earl himself, or the lady, of course," Noelle concluded, bringing the secretary back to earth. The Earl was not going to be happy.

* * *

"Back already, James? Did you have the pup delivered to Maringa?" When James tried to explain to his cousin about personalities and cat fanciers versus dog lovers, the Earl grew indignant.

"What kind of May game is this, James? You know I have that speech to prepare. Did they want more money? Is that it?"

"No, Justin. They seemed sincere about it."

"Come now, they must be running some kind of rig. What are they, climbers just wanting to meet the title? I have no time for mushrooms! Gads, they're not man hunters, are they? They'll catch cold at that."

"No, I really believe them. The younger one, Miss Ferne, does not want to part with the dogs at all, it seems. You should have seen her—with the puppies, I mean."

"Is she as beautiful as they say?" The Earl looked amused; his cousin blushed.

"An angel. I did ask if I could take her riding some afternoon, if that is all right with you."

"I suppose she turned you down, out for bigger game." The Earl was ready to take umbrage for the slur to his cousin-secretary-friend.

"No, you cynic. Miss Ferne said she would be delighted, right away. Asked me what day, even. None of those airs the chits are affecting."

"Are you so well up on debutantes, then? I thought I kept you too busy."

"Jus, you know I'm not in the marriage mart! Anyway, Miss Ferne is beautiful and . . . and innocent. Her sister even made sure the aunt would be along, for chaperone."

When the Earl saw how serious his younger cousin was about it, he refrained from further teasing. If the lad wanted to get himself leg-shackled to a penniless beauty, it would not help his political career any, but if the wind sat in that quarter . . . "What is the sister like, hm? I take it she is the one calling the tunes, not the aunt."

"Right. The aunt knits—sweaters for the dogs! She says they get cold during the winter. The sister, Miss Noelle, seems to have a head on her shoulders—quite attractive ones too, I might add. She started spouting Latin at me, a poem to a dog named Issa. Can you imagine writing a poem to a dog?''

''What, is she a bluestocking?''

''No, I don't suppose so. She just really cares about this Maltese breed. You've got to see for yourself. You're always saying how the only sport you still find interesting is watching people. Well, here's your chance.''

''You almost begin to intrigue me. If they are the same Armstrongs I am thinking of—Sterling, it was—I knew their father. What parties he used to give! Yes, I suppose I shall have to call on your beautiful Miss Ferne and her redoubtable sister, especially if I want any peace from Maringa.''

There was at least one other sport the Earl was still enthusiastic over, and if he chose to take his pleasure with a lady in the business, who was to blame him? After all, a great many of his married friends gave up a lot more, and received a lot less in return. If anyone had ever dared to ask the Earl where love entered into all this, he would most likely just give that slow, gentle smile of his and state that he must have had the malady as a child. He would have to ask his old nurse, but now he seemed to be unsusceptible. No, everyone paid one way or the other, the Earl had decided long ago; few could claim such rewards as Maringa Polieri. Admittedly, few could afford her.

When the Earl of Wrenthe took a mistress, it was accepted that she would be elegant, discreet and fully aware that this was a financial arrangement, to last only as long as both parties wished. No emotional crises, no jealous storms, no recriminations—for that he could get married! In return, the Earl was always generous and kind. He understood the plight of a woman dependent on her looks and on men. He was not one to cause the downfall of a woman, nor to demean her for it. If she made him happy, he would try to make her happy, thus the effort to purchase one of the Armstrong dogs.

Maringa Polieri was an exquisite Italian beauty of vivid colouring—black hair and eyes, lips of a red never found in nature—sumptuous proportions and ambitions. She knew she would never get Wrenthe to marry her; that was not even a consideration. No, when he left her sooner or later, and she meant it to be as much later as possible, she planned to have a respectable bank balance and, if not a respectable name, at least a well-known one. She wanted to be the most fashionable of the fashionable impures, the most expensive, the most desirable courtesan in all of England. That way *she* could pick and choose her next protector, not be at the mercy of the first man there to pay the bills. She did not expect to find another gentleman so generous, or so easy to please, or who pleased her so well. But if she had the time, and the leverage of notoriety, then who was to say she couldn't find some besotted old fool to marry her? Right now the height of modality seemed to be those fantastically expensive little dogs. They were a symbol to Maringa, and she wanted one.

La Polieri was much too wise in the ways of men to throw a scene for her imperturbable lord; there was nothing he would dislike more. When the dog was not forthcoming, however, it was difficult for one of her fiery temperament to maintain such a cool façade, but she still had her ways of getting what she wanted. Even mistresses could get headaches.

Two days later the Earl of Wrenthe rode to Chauncey Square. He left his horse in the care of a groom in ill-fitting livery, with a limp. It was not Wrenthe's nature to ignore human suffering, so he reached in his pocket for a coin, asking kindly, "Horse get you, lad?"

"Nay, sir, 'twere a piece of lead," the groom replied, touching his cap.

"Boney?"

The boy looked up and down the quiet street, then winked. "Excise men."

The Earl would have followed the groom down the alleyway to the stables, out of curiousity maybe, or just to make sure his horse actually arrived there, but the door to No. 4 was standing open, a familiar figure holding it.

"Taylor! By all that's holy, man! I heard you'd retired years ago." Lord Wrenthe took the butler's hand and shook it vigorously, a liberty even Winston would not have thought of taking with Taylor's dignity, for all that Taylor had put him on his first pony.

"My lord, it is a pleasure to see you also. I have returned to London to assist the Ambassador's children."

"So it is Sterling's family. Where were they? Derbyshire? I expect you'll be fixed with the young Viscount now?"

"No, my lord, Master Win—Lord Winston, that is—is a *country* gentleman." Taylor's face showed no expression, like a perfect butler, but his tone of voice said "snakes, slugs, sheep." Rather than seem disloyal he added, "He would do very well on the Town, but chooses to return to the property."

"Not like his father then?"

"Not like the Ambassador at all, except in looks."

"Ah, a waste for a man of your talents, Taylor. My butler Henesley is getting on, you know. I've been thinking of pensioning him off. I don't suppose—"

"No, my lord," Taylor said stiffly, looking straight ahead. "My ladies need me."

"What, the ubiquitous Taylor tied to apron strings? I would not have believed it! Do you recall the Ambassador's bashes? That time I challenged Minkle to a duel, but I was too foxed to stand up? I might have managed if he'd chosen pistols. He was such a bad shot we would neither of us have hit anything. But the fool chose swords. There I was, one hour till dawn, drunk as a . . . a lord. You and Sterling took me to the kitchen and put my head under the pump, then filled me with coffee. Yes, and made me presentable enough after to face my father. . . . Gads, I was green. I don't even remember what the duel was about."

"A woman, my lord," Taylor reminded him, thawed enough for a slight smile.

"It is *always* a woman, Taylor! Are you sure I cannot tempt you away from this respectable female stronghold?"

"No, my lord," Taylor said wistfully. "I couldn't leave the Ambassador's family, now could I?" As if to make up for this, Taylor added, "But I could put you onto a case of very fine brandy."

Wrenthe recalled the injured groom. "Taylor, I am with the Home Office now!"

"Oh, well, then make it two cases."

Both men laughed, the Earl's deep and hearty enough to be heard in the library, where Noelle had been going over accounts. Since this was not her favourite activity, she was happy enough to be distracted. She stepped into the hallway to find the source of such amusement. She saw a very dark gentleman of just over average height but superb build handing his beaver hat, gloves and riding crop over to Taylor, who was actually smiling!

The stranger was just now saying, "Taylor, if you can just get me one small dog, I would be satisfied for today."

Noelle stepped forward. "I believe I can help you there, sir, if I may be permitted."

The gentleman turned around quickly, a perfectly acceptable social smile fixed in place. When he saw Noelle, however, in a simple but well-filled gown of sprigged muslin, a green ribbon threaded through her auburn curls, green eyes filled with curiosity, then the smile grew. It started at one side of his mouth, spreading to the other, until his whole face seemed to come alive with a warmth missing before. He just said, "Ah."

Taylor coughed. "Quite. My lady, may I present his lordship, the Earl of Wrenthe. My lord, Miss Noelle Armstrong."

Noelle automatically curtseyed and held out her hand, but she was still watching the Earl's face. As he was recalled to his manners, the smile faded, leaving him a fairly severe expression. It was the heavy, unruly eyebrows, Noelle decided, almost meeting, and the three frown lines on his forehead that gave him that serious look. His dark-brown eyes under thick lashes remained admiring, little gold flecks sparkling. He was not exactly handsome, she felt—why, his nose did not seem quite straight!—but thoroughly, devastatingly attractive. Everything about the Earl spoke a degree of fineness: the wavy black hair with a few locks falling over his forehead, a touch of grey at the temples; the high chiselled cheekbones, strong chin and generous mouth; the way his coat of blue superfine stretched so well over broad shoulders; the buckskin breeches and high-polished boots; even his ease of manner. Now *here* was a gentleman. He was everything she wanted—for Ferne, of course.

"This way, if you would, my lord. Taylor, could we have tea in the Chinese room please."

As they walked down the hall, the Earl referred to his conversation with the butler: "I was privileged to know your father, Miss Armstrong. Taylor and I were reminiscing about a few moments of my youth when the Viscount helped me out of a hobble or two. The country lost a fine man when he passed on."

"Thank you, my lord. Did you know my mother also?"

"I may have, but I cannot recall. I was just down from Oxford when I first met Lord Sterling. I saw him mostly at the clubs, before he was sent abroad a great deal. Did your mother travel with him?"

"Very rarely. She preferred to stay at home. I am said to have her looks."

"Then I certainly never met her. I would have remembered that!"

Noelle was a little disappointed. Empty flattery, careless flirting were not what she could admire.

"Sincerely, Miss Armstrong," he said, holding the door for her.

Noelle blushed that her feelings must have shown on her face. Then she was even more annoyed with herself for acting like a schoolgirl. Get a hold on yourself, Nell, she demanded. He may be an Earl, and a fine looking man, but he is only here to buy a dog. With that, she was able to make the introductions in as dignified a manner as possible with two dogs prancing around for attention. Hattie put down her knitting and adjusted the spectacles; Ferne curtseyed prettily and coloured when Lord Wrenthe kissed her hand. For once Noelle felt a twinge of resentment, not because the Earl hadn't kissed her hand—she fully expected every man to be struck speechless at first sight of Ferne—but because Ferne could blush so adorably while Noelle merely looked and felt so awkward.

"Did Mr. Waverly tell you of the history of the Maltese breed, Lord Wrenthe?" she asked as they took their seats, getting the conversation back on proper course.

"Merely that it is very ancient and that you are quite knowledgeable about it. Would you mind repeating what you told him?"

Noelle *never* minded that, so she explained about Melites and Malta and how it was questionable exactly where the breed arose, and about Strabo and the Cambridge scholars. While she poured the tea, Ferne continued with the story of their mother's first pair in the Viscount's pockets. Ferne formally introduced Plato, who sat quietly by Noelle's chair, and Jasmine, who, as always, was begging for something to eat. The Earl listened attentively and smiled, so Noelle was encouraged.

"As you can see, we really care about our dogs, so it is important to us to make sure they have good homes. Mr. Waverly was unable to tell us about the lady who would actually own the dog." Noelle hoped she did not sound as vulgarly curious as she feared. "That is why we needed to see you in person."

"Does she really want it?" Ferne put in. "That is most important. We also need to know that she will give it proper grooming and enough exercise."

"Yes, and a little more about the lady herself," Noelle continued. "For instance, is she active or sedate; would she care if the dog were male or female?"

The Earl was quiet for a moment, but a smile danced across his face as if in some very private amusement. He must be very fond of the lady, Noelle thought naïvely, since the very thought of her makes him smile.

"Let's see. The—um—lady is a close personal friend of mine, a fairly recent association, so she is unacquainted as yet with James." He turned to Ferne, one corner of his mouth still twitching in a half-restrained grin as he spoke. "She most assuredly wants the dog; she made that very plain. As to my friend's—um—style, she does not have a wide circle of friends, nor does she get about much. The dog will be good company for her in those quiet times." Wrenthe was not purposely trying to delude his hostesses. One did not, after all, discuss one's mistress with gentlewomen, particularly such innocents as these. The roundaboutation he was employing was meant to protect their virginal ears, not deceive them. The oddness of the situation could not escape his admittedly quirky sense of humour, though. James had been right; he wasn't bored at all!

"As for which gender of dog, I can most assuredly swear to the lady's preference for males." Noelle still felt the Earl was thinking of his friend's partiality for himself, which was perfectly understandable—both her partiality and his knowing smile.

When Ferne left to retrieve the sole remaining male pup from the kitchen region, Noelle went to fetch the pedigree sheet and bill of sale, leaving the Earl to chat with Aunt Hattie. In the most civil manner, he inquired about her needlework.

"Your Mr. Waverly was interested too," she answered, a trifle flustered at so fine a gentleman's attention to such a mundane topic. Why couldn't he talk about the weather? "It will be cold before you know it, and little dogs can take a chill."

"Really? I would not have thought it, with all that hair."

"Well, they are not used to being out a lot. These are not kennel hounds, you know."

"Yes, I can see that. How many dogs do you have?"

"You would have to ask Nellie or Ferne. I sometimes cannot tell the little b—dears apart." Even Aunt Hattie was not immune to the half smile and understanding twinkle in the dark-brown eyes. Relaxing, she confided: "These little coats are just to keep my hand in until there are some grand-nieces and grand-nephews. Maybe I'll try making the dogs some booties to see if I remember how."

"Are you expecting these grand-babies soon?"

"You've seen the girls. What do you think?"

"Well, given the proprieties, you should not have to hurry, but yes, soon," was Wrenthe's answer, which seemed to delight the older woman. When Noelle returned it was to see the Earl laughing again, but his good humour was destined to be short-lived, as Noelle explained the contract to him.

"What, do you think I would mistreat any animal in my care?" One of those eyebrows was raised in a sure sign of affront. Noelle felt she had to persevere. Fools rush in, and all.

"No, my lord. If I thought so, I would not sell you the dog. This is a precaution merely, so that you are aware we would rather take the dog back than see it neglected."

"Very well," Wrenthe conceded, "I agree to your terms."

"Then will you sign here please?"

The Earl stood and took two steps toward Noelle, both eyebrows lowered, three lines etched deeper in his forehead, all traces of humour gone from his face. In barest civility he ground out: "Miss Armstrong, you are trying my patience. In fact, madam, if you were a man I would consider calling you out. I can only assume that in your abysmal naïveté you do not realise what an insulting remark you have just uttered. That or else you belong in Bedlam. I gave you my word, Miss Armstrong, the word of a *gentleman*. No Wrenthe has ever gone back on a promise."

Being glowered at by a very large angry person who has just implied his opinion that she might have feathers where her brains should be did not sit well with Nellie. Especially since the gentleman's ire had something to do with a starched-up view of that absurd entity, male honour. No one had ever before mistaken Noelle for a fool; no one had ever mistaken her for an even-mannered, demure miss who could be intimidated either. She stood and took two steps toward the Earl. More like chin-to-brass-button rather than eye-to-eye, but in a furious undervoice, she told him, "My father might not have been any high and mighty Earl, or some overdressed lordling, but he was a true nobleman, in every sense of the word. And it was *he* who taught me never to take a man's word. A man's word is as good as his intentions, my father always said, but his signature is acceptable in court."

"And I suppose your father would be proud of you now, haggling like some deuced cit in Trade?" the Earl sneered. The "high and mighty" rankled; so did the "overdressed," coming from some green-eyed chit whose curls were every-which-way out of their ribbon. "And asking an outrageous price besides."

"I am *not* in Trade. The Prince Regent buys and sells horses, yet no one accuses *him* of being in Trade. Don't earls try to make a profit when they sell their horses, and try to find good owners for them? My father used to say that a man who takes less than a thing is worth is either a good friend or a fool. As for the price, my lord, ladies spend a lot more on a presentation gown they will wear only once. The dog will be a loyal companion for many years. That should be worth any price."

The Earl had recovered from his pique and was beginning to see the humour in the situation. Losing his temper for the first time in ages, and to a green girl with freckles! He reached for the pen and ink. "You know, Miss Armstrong, I was fairly well acquainted with your father, and I do not recall him being quite so wise." He signed the certificate with a flourish: *Justin Gerald Waverly Wrenthor*.

Noelle's temper was the type that was cooled as soon as it was vented. She was also remembering her gay, devil-may-care father. Two dimples showed as she could not resist: "He also taught me never to trust a man with more than three names."

The Earl picked up the pen, drew a line through his previous signature and, giving Noelle a charming smile, scrawled *Wrenthe* across the page.

When they heard Taylor shut the front door, Ferne asked, "Did Papa really say all those things, Nellie?"

"Goose!"

"James, do you think you could take the carriage to Chauncey Square to pick up Maringa's pup and deliver it? Carefully, of course." The earl was sorting through the mail Waverly had left on his desk.

"Surely, Justin. You couldn't very well carry it on horseback."

"What, and get white dog hairs on my Bath superfine? My valet would never forgive me." At James's quizzical look the Earl relented. "No, the ladies thought the dog would be less upset, and I thought you would like the chance to call there."

"Wasn't I right in saying how they care about those dogs?" When Wrenthe absentmindedly agreed, making a notation in the margin of a letter, Waverly persisted: "Did you think she was as pretty as I said?"

"Pretty?" The Earl put the letter down and thought about it a moment. "No, I wouldn't say she was pretty at all. Too milk-and-water a phrase. Stunning, I'd say, or radiant, certainly prickly and exasperating, but definitely not pretty."

"Miss Ferne?" James asked in disbelief.

"Ferne? Who was talking about Ferne? She's pretty enough, I suppose, if you like beautiful widgeons."

=5=

A DAY IN THE PARK

A FEW DAYS later, Ferne and Winston were again in Hyde Park. It had rained that morning, so Ferne left her dog home, lest Jasmine get muddy footprints on her mistress's dress. It was the forget-me-not embroidered jonquil muslin from *Les Cousines*. With it Ferne carried a blue parasol with a yellow ruffle. She looked fine as fivepence, but it was wasted on the present company.

Win was gradually becoming friendly with other young men of similar tastes, simply by spending time at Tattersall's, the tailors and the carriage paths. These were the Bloods and the Tulips, young gentlemen about Town with nothing to do except entertain themselves, which they did by trying to outdo one another in every kind of sporting event or outlandish fashion. The Bloods were aspiring Corinthians, priding themselves on their neck-or-nothing sporting style. The Tulips were incipient dandies, dressed for fun, trying on affectations like new waistcoats. Both groups were highly addicted to gambling, it being the major occupation of the young men of the day. Winston had never had the opportunity to cultivate such a habit. His pockets did not run to wild excesses, nor was he about to ask his older sister to frank him. A fellow simply did not.

The group of sprigs standing around their curricles included some with striped waistcoats, yellow pantaloons and buttons as big as saucers; and some with neckcloths casually knotted, with sticking plaster over an eye from some escapade. They were all discussing a proposed race between two of the curricles, heatedly debating the course, the merits of both teams and drivers, and the odds anyone would give. Winston was hailed with "Here's Sterling. What's your opinion of Hanneford's greys?'' and ''Nice coat, old chap. I am backing Lockhardt. Ceddy Hanneford's the most cowhanded whipster I know.''

Horses, now, were something Winston knew. This was not like playing cards, where even Aunt Hattie, who had trouble remembering the day of the week, could trounce him. A race was something he would be willing to put his blunt on. ''What are the odds on the greys?'' he asked, leaving Ferne at the edge of the group.

It must be noted that while both groups of gentlemen shared an affinity for gaming, they also for the most part shared an aversion to women. They welcomed Win's sister very politely, the Tulips making their most elegant legs in acknowledgement of her beauty, and then they ignored her. To these young scions of the noble houses, females cried, sulked and schemed. They were something you were either related to or forced to dance with, certainly not as intriguing by light of day as Hanneford's new turnout.

A different attitude prevailed with a cluster of gentlemen on horseback gathered around a dashing high-perch phaeton a few yards away. These men, also from noble families, had those extra five or ten years to learn how indispensable the frailer sex was to their well-being. In this group, the experimenting was done, reputations were already made. The sportsmen were the real Corinthians, members of the Four Horse Club; the Fops, unless too *outré*, were now men of fashion, forsaking flamboyance for the quieter elegance of Brummell. These men were also habitual gamblers, preferring their clubs and even gaming dens, faro and piquet, to betting on chicken races or the colour of the next lady passerby's hat. These were, for the most part, men of substance, or substantial indebtedness by now, who had a taste for the finer things in life, such as women.

Ferne could not help noticing this, nor how those other men were paying a great deal of attention to the one woman in their midst, an exquisite raven-haired lady in a scarlet hussar-type outfit, seated in the phaeton. Ferne was not jealous of the other woman's looks, nor of the admiration she was receiving, but there was just enough vanity in her that she was miffed at being ignored. Besides, she was bored. What did she care who won some silly race, if both drivers didn't overturn their vehicles and break their necks? It was much more interesting to watch the other lady laugh at her beaus. One of the riders waved and moved away, giving Ferne a clear view of the woman's escort, the driver of the phaeton, the Earl of Wrenthe. Ferne was noting how well the couple looked together, both so dark, when the lady reached beside her and picked up a dog to show to one of the gentlemen on horseback. It was Jasmine's puppy and the lady was lifting it by its front legs! The puppy yelped; Ferne raced across the carriage path.

"No! No! You must never lift the puppy that way! You will hurt him, and ruin his bones."

There was a very shocked silence around her. The Earl, frowning, looked down and coldly told her, "Yes, we see. The dog is fine now, so you go back to your brother."

Ferne could not leave well enough alone, however, not when one of her dogs was in danger. This man, who had argued so heatedly with Nell, was now acting uncivilly towards her. Ferne was not sure he could be trusted with the dog after all.

"I am sorry, my lord, but you did say the dog would be well treated. Could I just show you how to lift a puppy correctly, Miss . . . ?"

The lady was smiling; the riders were laughing; the Earl was scowling furiously. There was this little dab of a chit, staring up at him in blue-eyed innocence, looking even smaller and younger amid the horses and their worldly riders. She was all strawberries and cream and springtime colours—and damned purity shining like a halo—waiting to be introduced to his mistress!

He very nearly growled out the names, so enraged was Wrenthe over this bit of awkwardness. While Ferne did, in fact, instruct Maringa in the proper handling of the Maltese, all the gentlemen listened politely. No one would dare even one snicker, such was the thunder in the Earl's face. Wrenthe was thinking how he would like to wring Ferne's beautiful little neck, or take his horsewhip to that ninny-hammer of a brother. *Some*one would pay for this. A man of his experience, trapped in a coil of such stupendous bad *ton*. One never even mentioned ladybirds in a real lady's presence; one certainly never introduced them, lest poor morals rub off, or were catching like measles. It simply was not done, except that he had just done it. At last, while Ferne was discoursing on how much and what to feed the dog, her brother arrived. He must have been hurriedly advised by his friends, for he was all red-faced and stammered an apology before dragging his sister away. And a thundering scold he was giving her, the Earl was pleased to hear. At least it would never happen again. The Earl decided he would save a few choice words of his own for the boy until later. Just let young Sterling get the clothhead out of the park before she turned into a watering pot, making the scene even worse.

Maringa was wearing a very satisfied little smile, like a cat in the cream. She was holding the dog, correctly, thank goodness, against her cheek in a very affecting pose.

"Dog lovers, don't you know," the Earl said to his friends as he gathered the reins of his team, ready to make another circuit of the park. "They are all fanatics."

"He what? He gave the dog to his mistress?" You might as well have said he ate it for breakfast. "To a . . . a. . ."

"A Cyprian, miss. A high-flyer." Taylor was always helpful.

"And then he let my sister talk to that . . ."

"Lightskirt, miss? Bit of muslin?"

"How dare he! Taylor, get the carriage.!"

"How dare he?" She was still fuming, pacing up and down the second-best drawing room in the Earl's Grosvenor Square mansion. She had been too furious to notice much, except that most of Aunt Sylvia's town house could fit into the black-and-white marbled hallway. When she had rushed out of her house, Ferne was still sobbing on Aunt Hattie's shoulder. Noelle had only paused to grab a pelisse, an old brown one that did not even match her dress, she realized disgustedly. Now she was being kept waiting, the butler said, while his lordship dressed.

"Fop," she said to herself. Except that the Earl picked that moment to enter the room, and she had said it out loud.

Wrenthe was dressed for a dinner party, black coat of perfect cut, white knee breeches on well-muscled thighs, white satin waistcoat, ruffles at his sleeves. *He* thought he looked complete to a shade. What did this curly-headed peagoose know about fashion anyway? When his man told him Miss Armstrong was calling, he'd prepared to soothe her agitated nerves, reassuring her and her aunt that no harm had been done. There was something about this woman, though, that was *not* soothing to him. In truth, he was already out of temper. Again.

"Well, another Miss Armstrong with no care for her reputation. Or were you not aware that a lady, and I emphasize *lady*, never calls alone at a gentleman's residence?" No polite courtesies here.

"I am not so sure this is one, *my lord*." Returned in kind. "But yes, I am aware. My brother is waiting outside. I wanted to speak to you alone, however, especially concerning 'reputations.'"

"Don't go off in a distempered freak, Miss Arm—"

"I am *not* in a distempered freak, Lord Wrenthe." She stamped her foot to prove it. "I only want to know how you dare treat other people's good names with so little disregard, such high-handedness, so—"

"If you would let me get a word in, Miss Armstrong, I might try to explain. As it is, I think the whole thing will blow over with no lasting damage. People will understand that Miss Ferne is just young and inexperienced, not wayward." The Earl felt this was a good, calm approach. He did not like these emotional scenes, or brangling with a woman, even one who looked so attractive, green eyes flashing. He thought he might now ring for tea.

"It won't wash, my lord. I want the dog back. You signed a guarantee that it would be treated well, and it is not so."

"What, because she picked it up wrong? Miss Armstrong, the dog is in excellent care, so you can get off your high horse over one little incident. I assure you it will be forgotten tomorrow, when some other faradiddle takes its place. Would you care for tea? Some Madeira, perhaps?"

His anger Noelle could respond to; she was angry, he should be, too. This amiability of his, this effort at polite conventions, was infuriating. How could she be in a rage alone? First he made her feel drab, now ill-mannered. If he tried to charm her with that smile of his, she thought, she would throw something. Luckily for the Meissen shepherdess near at hand, her next words knitted his eyebrows together again.

"I want the dog back, Lord Wrenthe," she said in a firm, rational tone of voice. "Because you have used it to damage my sister's good name, because the dog is with an uncaring owner. And because, my lord, you have misrepresented the case. That was no close lady friend of yours. You have given one of our dogs to a noted courtesan, to be part of her stock-in-trade. 'Lady of Quality' indeed! I give that"—a snap of her fingers—"for your gentleman's word."

"Miss Armstrong, you are the most rag-mannered female I know! It is clear now that you are no picture of innocence wronged, no diminished virtue come to demand retribution. Oh no. Now I see what you are: You are an ambitious snob. You only wanted the dogs to go to good owners—hah! You only wanted the mutts to go to *noble* owners, to prominent owners, to raise your own social standing. You are nothing but a climber, Miss Armstrong, so don't come to me with your self-righteous little nose in the air."

That same little nose—at least hers was straight—was starting to sniffle. Home truths hurt, but broken dreams hurt worse.

"Was it so wrong? Is it so terrible that I wanted to see my sister marry well? Have my brother make friends who aren't pig farmers? Can you understand that—you who know everybody and have everything—that I wanted them to have their rightful places in Polite Society? You are the snob, because you don't care about ruining other people's chances for happiness." She was weeping now.

The Earl mopped his forehead with his handkerchief, then quickly handed it to Noelle. "Please, Miss Armstrong, please sit and . . . and I'll call for tea. No? Well, then, why don't you take a moment to compose yourself." The Earl knew exactly how to deal with a lady in distress: throw water on her, call for her maid or kiss her. Since the situation did not look desperate enough for the water and there was no maid, and Wrenthe had an inkling he would get slapped if he followed his own inclination, the Earl tactfully withdrew. Before he left he did tell Noelle not to worry; he would right things with Ferne. "I'll just have a word with your brother before I send him in to you."

It was more than a word that the Earl had to say, after such an encounter. He put quite a flea in the young gentleman's ear, in fact, calling him a green fool, a nodcock and a gudgeon, among other things, who was to blame for the whole situation. Poor Win could only stand there shamefaced. Noelle had already given him a rare trimming, and he'd got *such* a look from Taylor. Now here was this out-and-outer, a regular nonesuch, making him feel like a schoolboy. The Earl was threatening to teach him better manners, the hard way. He would do it now, Wrenthe declared, except he did not want to wrinkle his clothes.

"Don't you doubt it, Sterling. If something like this happens again I'll have your head on a platter. In fact, you meet me at Gentleman Jackson's Boxing Salon tomorrow morning and I'll show you I mean what I say."

Winston could not believe he was about to get pulverized for such a minor, to him, offence, and all Ferne's doing anyway. He was about to remonstrate with the Earl when he noticed the other man was smiling, having finally taken pity on the youngster. Even Win was aware of the honour being conferred, a chance to go the distance with such an adept of the art. Gratified, he shook Wrenthe's hand.

"I'll see you there, my lord, but I had better warn you. We bumpkins know a thing or two about the fancy ourselves." He grinned. "Comes from that clean country living."

"I'll look forward to it, cawker. Now get your sister and get home. I'll be late for dinner as it is."

The Earl took his beaver hat from the butler and was adjusting it in the hall mirror. "You know, Henesley, I do not recall being riled as much all year as I have been in the one week I've known the Armstrongs. The damned shame is that I'll have to take them in hand somewhat, or it will be on my conscience. They have no more idea how to go on than kittens."

The hat was set at an exact angle on the wavy black curls, not tilted enough to be raffish, just jaunty. He reached for his gloves, turning to permit Henesley to drape a satin cape over his shoulders. "I owe it to the Ambassador, but it's going to be a blasted nuisance." With that he took up his cane and stepped out to the waiting carriage, whistling.

6

ANOTHER DAY, ANOTHER DILEMMA

THE EARL'S PLAN was simple. First he would meet young Sterling at Gentleman Jackson's. If, as he had no doubt, the lad shaped up well and gave a good accounting of himself, Wrenthe would take him over to White's. White's was that male stronghold where a gentleman could indulge in three of his favourite pastimes: gambling, drinking and ogling the women from its famed bow windows. There the Earl could introduce Winston around, especially to some of the older members, possibly friends of the late Viscount's who could be counted on to watch out for the youngster. Winston could meet the right sort there; he could gamble, if such was his pleasure, without danger of falling into the clutches of some Captain Sharp waiting to fleece an ignorant country lamb. With any luck, the young man would avoid the peep-o'-day boys too, if he stuck to the acquaintances he'd meet at White's. That would give his sister one less thing to worry about, her brother being taken up by the watch, or beaten in some back alley of a flash house. If relieving Miss Armstrong's mind was suddenly a paramount concern to Wrenthe, he only assumed it was some long-buried paternal instinct. After all, he was more than ten years older than Noelle, and he had always made it a policy not to get romantically involved with well-bred females. So his motives had to be pure . . . hadn't they? Damn those green eyes!

Well, the Earl decided, after he got Sterling squared away, he'd see about the sisters. See first off if Miss Noelle Armstrong was any kind of proper female. Not that he liked a giggling, simpering miss; he just needed to know that she could keep a civil tongue. The old social hens had vicious claws, and he was not about to volunteer for any more scenes. He might take the girls to Gunther's first, for an ice. If everything went smoothly, then he could drive them to the park and introduce them around, properly, this time. Sally Jersey was always holding court in Hyde Park; that old shrew Lady Strathwaite would be there too, with her ugly daughter and a lot of influence. The Earl knew he had ample social credit to dispel any talk of yesterday's hobble. It would not take much, the thing would be done and his responsibilities would be fulfilled. He could still read that paper on the corn laws . . . if he could only stop seeing that tantalizing smile of Noelle's. He was too old for this kind of nonsense!

He was too old to get into the ring with a man fifteen years his junior too, it turned out. Winston could never touch the Earl—Wrenthe had too much science for that—but after the match Wrenthe was near winded, and the boy was ready for another ten rounds. A game 'un, all right. He would be happy to take Winston to the club where the Earl for one could recover his strength over a glass or two.

It turned out to be considerably more than two glasses, as first Lord Makepiece, then Admiral Hayes and Brockton Luitt, then a whole parcel of late-middle-age gentlemen wanted to buy poor Sterling's son a drink and reminisce about the high old times. Some of the tales about the Ambassador seemed a bit spicy to be relating to a man's son, the Earl felt, and some of them seemed highly improbable, besides being improper. Old men, old wine and old stories, he reasoned, a combination not conducive to the niceties of the truth. Winston seemed to be taking it all in good form anyway, having heard most of the stories from Taylor, who had initiated the young lord into the ways of the world and French brandy one not-to-be-forgotten night recently.

"But you missed the one about the wine merchant's twin daughters." Winston had them all chortling as he related a most apocryphal version. "It was before he met my mother, of course," he finished, showing due respect for whatever proprieties were left, before draining his glass. The older men, some still with powdered hair, were wiping tears from their eyes from laughing so hard. Winston would do, he would be fine on the Town, the Earl believed, which should please Miss Armstrong, and just possibly change her poor opinion of himself. Unless, that is, the Earl and Taylor were not able to smuggle Winston to his own room without Noelle's noticing how foxed her brother was. It would be just like that infuriating female to blame *him*.

No backstairs measures were necessary. The Viscount seemed to straighten up in the fresh air, and Noelle was not at home. She and her aunt were out visiting, explained a strange footman with one eye swollen shut. The Earl lifted his quizzing glass, the better to see the remarkable colours of the man's face. After his experiences with Taylor and the limping groom, Wrenthe did not dare inquire into anything to do with the Armstrongs' extraordinary staff. The footman returned a grin and said that Taylor was on a personal errand but Miss Ferne was at home. Would his lordship care to see her? His lordship would really rather not, but he felt that since he was here now, he had better make the most of it. His tiger was walking the horses; he'd be an adequate chaperone, for all he was just a half-grown boy, as was the fashion for men's coaches. A full-size groom would look foolish clinging to the back of the seat. Wrenthe had the footman take a message that he would be honoured if Miss Ferne would go for a drive with him, evidence that the Earl's head was none too clear either.

Ferne absolutely, positively did not wish to go for a ride with the Earl. He was always looking like thunderclouds or shouting at Nellie. Clarice was forever saying he was top-of-the-trees and she would give up a month's desserts to dance with him, broken leg and all, but Ferne just found him awesome. So she accepted the invitation, telling the messenger she would just be a minute changing her dress. Her reasoning was typically Ferne: Noelle, Aunt Hattie, even Winston, had repeated that it was of the utmost importance to be seen with only the best people, not ladies with smoky reputations. Everyone said the Earl was top drawer. Therefore, it should make them all happy if she was in his company, even if she were miserable.

She liked Winnie's friends much better. So what if they sometimes ignored her? They did not stare right through her!

But Nellie said that even if they came to call, or took her for rides, no man was going to marry a girl he never danced with. The Armstrongs were not being invited to any of the balls where these young men could be found. Aunt Hattie's friends were starting to ask them places, it was true, but mostly to musicales or afternoon teas or card parties, where every man was over fifty. At least they did not scowl at Ferne. Nellie's heart was on Almack's, though, and Nellie had said the Earl could help, if he wanted to. So Ferne took out her yellow merino. No, the pink muslin. What about the French cambric with blue stripes?

If Taylor were home, he would have offered the gentleman a brandy while he waited, and waited. Then again, if Taylor were home, he would have made Miss Ferne's excuses rather than permit her to go off with the Earl. Not that Taylor mistrusted Wrenthe, merely that disasters frequently occurred in Miss Ferne's vicinity, and the family could not afford another setback. Taylor was out on private business, though. He was making inquiries of the daytime habitues of The Duck and the Drake, having drawn a blank with the usual late-evening crowd of butlers, valets and footmen. Sam, the coachman from Derbyshire, had done some specialized driving for Taylor one night. What Sam wanted in exchange for his silent cooperation was the use of Taylor's network of information to track down his own love, Peggoty Gallagher, who had come to London to work in a fine lady's house. Sam had already made the rounds of placement bureaus, with no luck. One of the footmen had expressed his opinion of what type of house a green country girl could find work in; this was the man with darkened daylights who had held the door for Wrenthe. Sam had spoken through a split lip: "Nay, my Peg's a good girl. You be a sport there, Mr. Taylor, and ask some of your friends as work in the swells' houses. She's a handsome lass with bright-red braids and a chipped front tooth and nice round hips and . . ." To the dismay of his niece Moira, who was hoping Sam would forget about the bird in the bush, Taylor had agreed to help. With no results from the butler so far, and just to be on the safe side, Sam was spending a lot of his free time visiting certain dubious addresses, asking for his Peggoty. ("Sure we have a Peg, and a Polly and a Pam. Take your pick!")

*   *   *

Here Noelle thought she would only have to worry about her sister's reputation. Why, at any minute her starchy, sniffy and well-loved butler could be clapped in irons for free trading, and her trusted coachman in his shiny new livery was—Well, the less said about Sam's activities the better, except that the whole family was concerned about his evident distress. How could Noelle enjoy a carriage ride when the driver had dark circles under his eyes and moaned?

As if she did not have enough to fret over, the ancient, snuff-covered gentleman seated next to her kept trying to rub her foot with his. Noelle was miserably attending a lecture on the music of the spheres in Shakespeare and Milton, with accompaniments, by a very small gentleman with a whispery voice, his even smaller wife and a harp. The invitation had come through one of Aunt Hattie's "contacts." Noelle was the youngest person there by about thirty years and one of the few, other than the randy old relic next to her, who was not snoring. She edged her seat closer to her aunt's, vowing that she would be nibbled to death by ducks before she put herself in such a place again.

The words may have been different, certainly more colourful, but the sentiments were the same. The Earl was wearing a hole in Aunt Sylvia's attic Aubusson rug. He had already had two conversations with an ankle-high dog. Damned if he knew which one; the thing had so much hair he couldn't even tell its particulars. He had already consumed three stale bonbons, most likely the reason the dog could not be tempted to eat one. Now he was seriously considering developing a sudden malady, leprosy maybe, to get himself out of this house. He was an Earl, by Jupiter, with affluence and influence at Court. If that wasn't enough to keep him from such damnable situations, he thought furiously, what good was it all?

Then Ferne appeared, looking like a moon-struck poet's vision of eternal springtime, blushing prettily and apologising for keeping his horses standing.

"Not at all, Miss Ferne, my groom has been walking them," he said, taking her arm. His heart may not have melted entirely at the sight of such sweet beauty; still and all, he was only a man. Her peach muslin gown showed her delightfully girlish figure to perfection, in an obviously expensive example of good taste, quality workmanship and the height of fashion. The Earl knew a great deal about women's clothes, having paid for more than a few wardrobes in his time. Connoisseur that he was, he could recognize artifice, as opposed to artful enhancement, which latter was the case here. All in all, he decided as he handed her up to his phaeton, he would be pleased to have Miss Ferne ride beside him, proud to introduce her around. But once he had taken the reins from his tiger and started the team into the traffic, a new problem arose: What do you say to a chit almost young enough to be your daughter? He complimented her on being in looks; she blushed. He noted that it was a lovely day; she nodded. He certainly was not going to take her to sit mumchance at Gunther's for an hour, but he had an inspiration.

"Did you ever hear the tale of Lady Ringthorpe's pugs at Gunther's?"

Success. Her delightful face turned up to him eagerly. "No, what about them?"

"Well, Lady Ringthorpe—have you ever heard of her?" When Ferne shook her head he was relieved, but did some rapid editing in his head. It was hard to remember how very innocent Miss Ferne was. "She was a rather . . . um . . . dashing widow, but she was received everywhere. She used to like to have her dogs with her, two pugs they were, always wheezing and looking like their eyes would fall out if you petted them too hard. One day a gentleman friend took Lady Ringthorpe to Gunther's and she insisted that her darlings could not wait in the carriage alone, so they all went in. Now her friend was a very well-known gentleman, very high in the government, you see, and the waiter was afraid to offend him. So they all sat down in chairs around a table, the man, the lady and the two dogs. You can imagine the reactions of the other patrons, especially when Lady Ringthorpe ordered an ice for each of the pugs. It was absolutely silent. You could hear the dogs slobbering over the dishes."

Ferne was already giggling. "And what happend then?"

"Then, when they were finished, the waiter, very courteous

and refined—you know the type—lifted the dogs' dishes with the edge of a cloth, placed the dishes and the cloth on his tray and marched through the room like a soldier on dress parade. He threw the whole thing out the door, marched back and said, 'Will there be anything else, my lord?' ''

"Oh, I can just see it," Ferne said, laughing, two adorable dimples showing. "How silly of Lady Ringthorpe! Did they ever let her in again?"

"I am not certain about that, but I do know that they put a little plaque near the door saying that pets were not permitted."

After that, conversation went on more smoothly as Ferne relaxed. The Earl was not as grim as he'd seemed, she decided. Maybe that was why such a gorgeous creature as yesterday's lady wanted to be his mistress. Even Ferne knew better than to express *that* opinion out loud—she did not need Noelle to tell her how to go on all of the time—so she said nothing.

The Earl's meagre wealth of dog stories was running out with some distance to the park still to go.

"How does it happen that you were home alone on such a lovely afternoon?" he ventured.

"I was supposed to spend the day with my friend Clarice—Clarice Kingsley, that is. She is not Out yet, so I daresay you don't know her." The Earl solemnly confirmed this, without revealing that he knew almost no females under the age of consent, especially debutantes. Once started, Ferne chattered like a magpie, telling all about Clarice's broken leg—"Her brother dared her, you see"—and what pleasure the new puppy was giving her.

"She can't walk it, of course, but her maid is very good about that." And Ferne went on, until she finished, "But her mother sent over a note this morning saying that Clarice would be better resting today, so could I visit another time instead."

The Earl heard the disappointment, maybe even hurt, and thought he knew the cause. Lady Kingsley, known to be a strict moralist, must have got wind of Ferne's encounter with Maringa. She would not want her precious chick to be painted with the same brush, so to speak, so was cutting the connection. The Earl's mouth tightened, his brow furrowed; he was even more determined to smooth Ferne's path. A silly error, that was all. He would show the *ton* the girl was no more improper than a pansy. One talk with her and even the starchiest matron would be convinced of the girl's sweetness.

While the Earl was thinking, he was frowning. Ferne was afraid she had done something to displease him again, this gentleman of decidedly uncertain temper, so she nervously tried to make conversation, to restore the former easy relationship.

"Do you ever visit whore houses, my lord?"

That brought him around quickly. His sudden movement sawed at his horses' mouths like a veritable novice, and the high-bred chestnuts took exception, so it was some moments before the Earl could give Ferne his full attention.

"Do I ever *what*?" he almost shouted, checking over his shoulder to see the cheeky grin on his tiger, up behind. In a hoarse whisper he stopped her: "No, don't say it again. Don't *ever* say it. Don't even think it, for that matter. Young ladies are not even supposed to know such places exist."

"But Winnie told me all about them."

The Earl muttered something about how he should have murdered the gudgeon that morning while he had him in the ring. "*I* am not your brother, Miss Ferne. I am not even related to you, thanks be, so you must not discuss these things, I beg of you."

"But you were being so nice, and Win said you know everything—"

Dear Lord in heaven, Wrenthe asked himself, what did I ever do to deserve this? He tried very hard to get a rein on his emotions—he had been getting a lot of practise with that lately—and suggested that Ferne not try to explain further.

"Very well, but Sam is at . . . one of those places . . . all the time and Win said he would go help. But Nell says we should try other ways to find Peggoty."

"Peggoty?" the Earl asked weakly.

"Peggoty Gallagher, from Derbyshire. Her father is a farmer, except Noelle thinks he does more poaching than plowing. Anyway, Peggoty and Sam were keeping company but they had an argument, over Jennie Campbell, I believe, but you won't care about that. And Peg left. She said she was going to work for a grand lady in London, and moved out. Sam has been looking for her at all the employment offices since we came to Town. Now he is in sad form because Taylor can't find anything about her and someone told him she was most likely working at a . . . you know what.''

The Earl was attempting to follow this rambling story while threading his team through the crowded gates of Hyde Park and onto the congested carriage path.

''Why doesn't he contact her father again? Maybe there has been word by now,'' he suggested helpfully, still wondering for what sins he was now being punished.

''That wouldn't work. Mr. Gallagher cannot read, and Pegotty cannot write.''

''Can Sam write?'' The Earl was playing for time, wondering where he came into the scheme. If this flea brain thought he would help search London's fleshpots for this Peggoty person, she was even more screw-loose than he had first thought, if that were possible.

''Nellie taught Sam to write, and all the other tenants' children.''

''She did? Isn't that unusual?''

''Well, she said that since we couldn't make all the repairs on their farms—we were very behind things, you know, after Papa died—that it was up to us to give our people *some*thing. A way of bettering themselves, she said. I can't see where it's helping Sam better himself, not in a —''

The Earl coughed. ''I bet Sam's . . . ah, Peggoty . . . has a good position in a proper home, as she said, parlourmaid or something very respectable, only it must be a small household, or not quite in London, so it will take longer to find her.'' Wrenthe was pleased to note that his cheery opinion had brought a smile back to Ferne's face, now they were in the middle of the park. Ladies did not usually look so disturbed in his company. ''I can make some inquiries if you like; I'm sure she will turn up.''

''Oh would you? That's ever so kind!'' Her smile was like the sun coming out on a cloudy day. The Earl was glad for his political training: Be sincere, one of his mentors had advised, even when you don't mean it. In general, Wrenthe did not approve of subterfuge, but if it made the girl happier to think the wench respectable, no harm was done. And he could get Henesley to ask around. But one girl in all of London? Right now his purpose was to establish *this* one respectably, and quickly, then get back to the business of government, the corn laws in particular. He directed his team to where Sally Jersey usually parked her brougham when receiving her admirers.

On the way, however, a young man of sporting blood started to pass them in his racing curricle. The Earl was holding his horses to a sedate walk, appropriate to the congested path; the young gentleman was not. The Earl's carriage horses were chosen for stamina, strength, speed and class. The other's were chosen for spirit and show. Which meant that when the fellow caught sight of Ferne and decided he needed a closer look, suddenly reining in his team to match the Earl's slower pace, his high-steppers took affront. One shied up; the other tried to pull ahead of the annoying restraint. The light curricle slewed around, grazing the Earl's carriage, but giving the other driver enough of a jolt that he jerked even harder on his ribbons. Suddenly there were horses bucking and snorting and kicking, grooms running and maidens screaming, by way of contributing to the chaos.

With quiet eloquence, the Earl was describing the younger man's parentage, his personal habits and various anatomical impossibilities, meanwhile regaining control of his own team. As soon as this was done and the tiger had their heads, Wrenthe leaped out of the phaeton and ran back to the other carriage, whose horses were still pawing the air and rolling their eyes. The Earl grasped their halters and firmed them to a standstill, although they were still quivering. When a groom came to hold them, Wrenthe directed his attention to the driver, now deathly pale over his spotted neckcloth and also trembling, as well he might. The Earl glanced quickly back at Ferne to see that she was unhurt. She was not hysterical at any rate, so he at least had that to be thankful for. The unfortunate whipster, vaguely known to the Earl as Cholly Wilburforce's younger brother, felt he'd best stay in his seat; the Earl felt otherwise. Young Wilburforce scrambled down, his arm in an iron vise.

He was thus silently escorted to survey the damage to the Earl's brightwork, the tiger assuring Wrenthe the horses had no pulls or sprains, at which Wilburforce decided it was safe to breathe again. His arm still in his lordship's grip, the two men next inspected Wilburforce's team and carriage, which had definitely received the heaviest damage. Still, Wrenthe said almost nothing, even smiling to the crowd that had gathered, assuring them that all was well, no one was harmed, they could continue their strolls, nice day wasn't it? If it were not for the fact that his arm no longer hurt—it had gone numb under Wrenthe's pressure—Wilburforce could almost believe he would live to see his twenty-first birthday. Hope died as the Earl led him towards a line of shrubbery, away from any casual observers, or possible rescuers, depending on one's viewpoint.

Ferne was not upset over the accident, nor injured in the slightest. When the Earl's fluent mutterings had reached the point of describing just where young Wilburforce's brains were located, however—just about the only thing, thankfully, she had understood—Ferne clasped her hands over her ears in horror. This naturally caused her parasol to fall over the side of the carriage. Now a high-perch phaeton might be an elegant showcase for a man's ability with a whip, but it was no ladies' vehicle. There was absolutely no way for her to get down without showing a great deal of stocking, except by being lifted out. And Wrenthe was in some bushes with the unfortunate young man, and the tiger could not leave the horses. What if Lord Wrenthe was a long while—though what the two men had to discuss in private was beyond her—and she just had to sit there waiting, in the sun? Maybe she would get freckles like poor Nellie!

She was looking forlornly down at her ruffled parasol when a man's voice asked, "Can I help you, ma'am? I recognized Wrenthe's carriage. I'm a friend of his, Sir Rupert Dynhoff, at your service."

Ferne looked up to see a gentleman on horseback. That he was a gentleman was obvious: the clothes, cultured voice and comfortable way he sat the bay stallion, plus the way he came to her aid. And he was a friend of the Earl's. So Ferne explained about the accident, the Earl off behind some trees, her parasol—and what was she to do? The stranger dismounted, said, "Permit me," then quite masterfully grasped her waist and lifted her down. Ferne smiled her thanks, although she had only wanted her parasol handed up, but one could not be impolite to a Good Samaritan, could one? So she expressed her gratitude again and shyly gave her own name. Sir Rupert took her hand and raised it to his lips. Ferne blushed. She just couldn't help it, so many people were looking. The gentleman seemed amused, but Ferne could not be sure. His face wasn't open, like Winnie's, or even expressive, like the Earl's. Sir Rupert was smiling, but his eyes were not somehow. About Wrenthe's age, she guessed, Dynhoff had more lines on his face. He was light-haired and very pale. He looked tired or sickly or disappointed, but maybe it was just his eyes again, Ferne granted charitably. They were a soft blue but the lashes were too pale, giving him a red-rimmed, watery look. Still, he was a friend of the Earl's. He must be, since he seemed determined to stay by her until Wrenthe returned.

To set her at ease, Dynhoff took Ferne's arm and led her a little away from the carriage, leading his horse behind them. He asked about Ferne's home and her visit to London. Ferne was delighted to tell him about her family, how they had received a wonderful inheritance from Aunt Sylvia, and the crocodile furniture and the dogs. She felt they were getting on famously; Noelle would be pleased she'd met another London beau.

Wrenthe, meanwhile, had fairly easily convinced Wilburforce that country air would benefit his health. The young man had quickly agreed, suddenly recalling how much there was to do on the estate. It would be a shame to miss the Season, but his mother'd be happy to have him home so he'd just be off, packing and all.

Straightening his cravat, the Earl walked back towards the carriage. He caught sight of Lady Strathwaite and her fubsy-faced daughter on their promenade, so the day was not a total loss. He'd just fetch Miss Ferne—

There was his carriage, nobody in it. His heart sinking, the Earl looked around. Sure enough, at some distance away, away from the chaperonage of the groom, Ferne was strolling with a man. Laughing at him, chatting with him. Not just any man, of course, either. No, it had to be Sir Rupert Dynhoff, the least suitable man in town. As the Earl hurried up to them, he could hear Ferne ask one of London's most notorious rakes, in her clear, sweet, *carrying* voice, "Sir Rupert, do you know anything about parlour maids?"

=7=

NOELLE AND THE EARL

"HENESLEY, DO YOU know Sir Rupert Dynhoff?" the Earl asked his butler a little later.

"A dirty dish, sir, so I am led to believe."

"A basket-scrambler, in fact? A rake and a bounder?"

"Quite so, my lord, yet still accepted in Society, since the Prince enjoys his company, I think."

"And one may assume this is common knowledge?"

"I should think so, Lord Justin. If I might inquire . . . ?"

"I seem to be responsible for Dynhoff's introduction to a young lady in my care, a very innocent young lady."

"Oh dear. Shall we expect another call from the young lady's sister, then, sir?"

"I fear so. I shall be in the library, Henesley, preparing."

"Shall I send in the sherry, my lord?"

"Precisely." There went the corn laws.

Fire wasn't quite sparking from Noelle's green eyes; smoke wasn't quite billowing from her nose . . . but almost, she was that mad. She was standing across the oak-topped desk from the Earl, waving one small fist in his face, shouting. A perfect lady.

"It wasn't enough that you introduce my sister to your . . . your paramour. No, then you take her out with no more chaperone than a half-grown boy, a stablehand! So it looks to all the world like you are setting her up as your next flirt. Taking her to the park to show off in front of half the *ton*. You might as well have published your intentions in the *Gazette*! Was that enough? Had the great Lord Wrenthe played wily-beguiled with our lives sufficiently? Oh no, not you. You had to surpass even your own boundless idiocy! Leaving her alone with Dynhoff! His reputation doesn't bear looking at, this friend of yours. This is a man you would let near a seventeen-year-old? You unconscionable cad! I *wish* I were a man. I'd . . . I'd . . .''

The Earl was, with effort and the two glasses of sherry he'd had time to down, maintaining his composure under fire. ''Won't you please sit down, Miss Armstrong? It was unfortunate—''

''Unfortunate? Is that what you call it? Unfortunate that my sister is ruined, that no man will ever make her an offer—an honourable offer, that is. Don't you feel that's a little more serious than 'unfortunate'?'' Noelle had jumped up to express herself more vigorously. ''You have the morals of a toad, sir, and at that the toad would be offended!''

The Earl, also standing now, commented drily, ''Now isn't *that* an elegant turn of phrase. I suppose you learned it in diplomatic circles?'' That unruffled exterior of his was beginning to crumble a bit. ''If you would just have a seat, I would try to help—''

''Sir, I beg leave to tell you,'' Noelle said, sitting primly, ''that if I had a choice between your help and the devil's, I'd start sewing little red slippers. You have been a big enough help as it is. The only assistance I want from you, the only aid I would accept, is that you leave us alone!''

She was on her feet again, headed towards the door. The Earl stood too, and that was the last straw, hopping up and down because no gentleman stayed seated while a lady stood. Some lady! He had had a rough enough day. A sleepless night haunted by green-eyed temptresses, the workout with Winston, a few hours of midday drinking, a carriage accident and a bumblebath in the park, and now this—again. He was tired and he was aggravated past bearing. She wanted it with no bark on it, did she? He grabbed her arm and shoved her into the chair.

''You just sit down and stay down. And you listen. It wasn't I who made micefeet of this affair, not by myself, not by a long shot. First off, Dynhoff is no friend of mine. He is someone I play cards with occasionally, and reluctantly. And if your peagoose of a sister had stayed where she was supposed to, nobody would have remarked on it. She is *forever* getting into scrapes, so you can just stop blaming me. She even asked me if I frequent . . . um . . . houses of ill repute.''

"Do you?" Noelle sniffed, but she stayed seated.

"That is not the point!" the Earl, pushed past endurance, shouted. Then, on reflection, he added, "Your estimation of my character continues to amaze me: I beat dogs, renege on promises, ravish maidens and most likely have the pox. Well too bad, madam. You'll just have to put up with me, pox and all. You'd have to be a perfect cabbagehead to think you could breeze through this alone, or to think I would let you to go out and darken *my* name. I do have some pride, Miss Armstrong. You are not the only one, you know . . . or do you want to talk about a surfeit of pride? About how you could have gone to your father's old friends, written to your mother's acquaintances, but no, you had to go your own way. You did not want to ask for help, right? Well that is pride, Miss Armstrong, and where has that taken you? You've got a diamond on your hands who attracts trouble like bees to honey, and you are not up to snuff to see her established. You're at *point non plus*, Miss Prim and Proper, and like it or not, you are going to get my help, no matter what you think of me.''

By this time, of course, Noelle's chin was starting to quiver.

"Damn, damn, damn!" How could one small woman bring out the worst in him, and so often? The Earl walked to the other side of the desk, his back to Noelle, so he would not have to see those eyes fill up. He poured himself a sherry, but could still hear her sniffling. He turned to offer her his handkerchief, again.

"I'll have to get my man to lay in a new supply," he tried. It did not work; a tear trickled down her cheek. Those wayward intentions of his were getting the better hand. It was all he could do not to gather her in his arms and— He'd better not dwell on that.

"Please, Miss Armstrong, please don't cry. I know I am a brute and I apologise for shouting at you. It's my damned —dashed—temper. But please don't cry.''

She snuffled into the cloth. "Papa always said it was taking unfair advantage, like cheating at cards. He used to say crying was a woman's second most effective weapon—oh.'' She blushed, realising too late what she'd just said.

"Now *that* I can imagine your father saying." He smiled at her, that slow-spreading smile that had time to warm her down to her toes. "Here, have a sip of sherry while we see about making a respectable woman of your sister."

Noelle hiccoughed once before tasting the wine. "I . . . I am not always such a shrew, honestly. Mama used to tell me it was the Wycombe auburn hair that gave me such a temper. She was the sweetest creature in nature, until someone threatened her family. Once some boys were teasing Win and she told him to work things out himself. Then three big boys started to hit him, all at once. You should have seen Mama, with her parasol and her reticule, going at those boys, right there on the village street. She was so mad she went to each boy's father and told them their sons were bullies who would end in Newgate if not taught some manners. Then she went home and had the vapours for a week. So . . . so you see, I must have inherited my deplorable temper. And I have been looking out for Ferne for so long, I just couldn't bear to see anything happen to her.''

"And I too have been regrettably hot-at-hand. Brummell always says not to apologise, as it lowers one's dignity, yet somehow we seem to bring out the beast in each other. May we not cry *pax* and shake hands? I really think we need to work together to fix this coil.''

Noelle smiled and shyly held out her hand to his firm grip.

"Fine, except for one small thing. You didn't by any chance come here alone, did you?" Could he stand being accused of compromising two ladies in one afternoon?

"No, Lord Wrenthe, Taylor is waiting. I went to get Winston, but he was sleeping too soundly to awaken." There was a hint of suspicion in her voice that Wrenthe chose to ignore, just as he ignored the fact that proper young women did not go about with their butlers in attendance.

"Good. Now, are there any more puppies left to sell?"

Whatever tension may have remained between the two disappeared into laughter as Noelle described the last and final sale.

"Do you know Lady Sheehan?" Noelle asked with a delicious giggle.

"That old quiz? She's as mad as MacDougal's aunt."

"But Taylor remembered her as being very wealthy and influential, if a trifle eccentric."

"She may have been simply eccentric years ago, but now she is definitely queer in the attic. She hardly ever leaves her house, I understand, and the family has a keeper for her."

"A very nice woman, Mrs. Brown, who owns spaniels. Lady Sheehan invited us all—Aunt Hattie, Ferne, myself, plus Plato and Jasmine—to tea next week with Mrs. Brown, the spaniels and Blossom."

"Blossom?"

"We explained how our male dogs were named after philosophers and the females for flowers, so Blossom it is. It's Blossom who wanted all her friends at her gathering, in fact. Lady Sheehan made that very clear."

"Lord, what an introduction to Polite Society that will be!" Wrenthe could not help laughing at the mind-picture of a tea party for canines.

"I think the dog will be good for the lady anyway, and she certainly adores it, so—"

"So the dogs are gone without much advantage. Old Taylor must be losing his touch."

"I fear he has his mind on a few other things," Noelle admitted, but volunteered no further information. The Earl had his own ideas, but kept mum in case Noelle was ignorant of Taylor's outside activities. Both were thinking that something had to be done about that situation also.

"Well, it seems we are going to have to work a little harder then," the Earl told Noelle, "but trust me, we'll muddle through."

Surprisingly enough, in view of their past dealing, Noelle did trust him. He told her the situation was not as desperate as it seemed; she believed him. He said he needed a few days to make some arrangements; she said she could wait.

She should be relieved, Noelle told herself miserably on the carriage ride home, that the Earl of Wrenthe was going to come to their aid. He was one of the Social lights, a true nonpareil, and he was going to introduce the Armstrongs to his friends. He was one of the busiest, most sought-after men in London, and he was going to take time to help them. Noelle should have been so happy. So why did she feel like she'd just swallowed a cast-iron doorstop? Because this fine gentleman, always courteous, always friendly—to everyone but her—also never exerted himself for others, never let himself get embroiled in scandalous situations, never, ever, associated with young, marriageable girls. He did not affect the boredom of the Carlton House set, with the studied drawls and condescending manners; he simply had nothing to do with anything dull or second-rate or provoking. Now he was about to change all that. Now, in spite of her lack of dowry and social standing, he was attracted enough to sweet-and-gentle Ferne to want to establish her properly, to introduce her to his mother, he'd even said.

It all meant one thing to Noelle: The stalwart bachelor had finally succumbed, and to a beautiful peahen. Noelle was delighted. It was everything she could have hoped for.

Like two cast-iron doorstops for dinner.

=8=

THE LORD AND THE LAPDOG

THE ARMSTRONG WOMEN spent the following afternoon on an excursion to Windsor Castle. They rode in the Earl's brougham, driven by his coachman and escorted by his secretary, James Waverly, who was a knowledgeable guide and an unexceptionable companion. Aunt Hattie was only disappointed that Mr. Waverly could not tell her if the rumours about the King were true, if he really spoke to angels. Ferne thought the monarch ought to have a dog, recalling how the old scholars had called the Maltese "the Comforter." Besides, if the King talked to the dog, no one would think he was so balmy. To Noelle, it was a pleasure to consider poor King George's problems instead of her own. It was a lovely outing, even nicer for being away from the staring, speculative eyes of Town. Noelle had begun to feel her every step was being scrutinised, judged—and found wanting. Why, even the air was cleaner here.

The Earl, meanwhile, was attending to business. Not the nation's, or his own vast financial holdings, but the very serious business of pleasure. His first stop was at Rundell and Bridges, the Bond Street jewelers, where he instructed his tiger to walk the horses out of the traffic for a while. All of the clerks being occupied, Wrenthe strolled about, looking at the velvet-lined cases. An elegant topaz-inlaid snuff box caught his fancy, then near the pearls a double string of green jade beads attracted him. Those eyes were that color green, he thought, somewhat smoky, not brilliant like emeralds, but with more depth. How the soft lustre of the ancient jade would shine against her smooth, alabaster skin. . . . He was startled from his reverie by a clerk asking if he could be of assistance.

"I would like to see something in diamonds, a bracelet, I think." The man offered a tray of thin pavé links, not at all what the Earl had in mind. "Heavier, um, more eye-catching. Extravagant, I suppose."

The clerk disappeared into the curtained-off portion of the shop. One of the owners returned, smiling in recognition of one of his wealthiest patrons. He carried a small box in which nested a bracelet with so many diamonds you would not be surprised to see a dragon guarding it. To the Earl the thing looked so heavy that a woman would need all her strength just to raise the arm wearing it. She would have to wear green-tinted spectacles not to be blinded by it. All in all, the most spectacularly vulgar thing he had ever seen.

"Perfect. I'll take it." It was not the most expensive piece in the shop, not that the Earl asked, only the fifth or sixth dearest. The Earl placed the box in an inner pocket, gave a last regretful look at the jade beads and left. The clerk held the door, the owner bowed him out, almost touching his nose to the floor.

Wrenthe's next stop was at a very neat little residence off King Street. Again the tiger was told to walk the horses so they didn't take a chill. His lordship chose not to see the insolent grin on his servant's face.

"*Caro mio*, how wonderful to see you. I did not expect you to call until later. You could not stay away, no?"

Maringa Polieri had been busy doing what she did best: looking seductive, just in case. Reclining on a daybed with a glass of wine and a French novel, she'd had the shades pulled against the harsh afternoon light. She was haloed in candle-glow, a black-haired siren in a flesh-coloured peignoir set with a dyed-to-match ostrich feather ruffle at collar and hem. An exotic bird indeed, she rose slowly from the divan as the maid announced him, opening her arms, and hence her robe, for his embrace. He could feel the warm flesh beneath his hands, breathe in the heady aroma of her scent . . . get a mouthful of feathers. The courtship ritual was interrupted as, coughing, he remembered his mission and stepped back a pace. Maringa puffed out her lower lip in a pretend pout, then resumed her position, making sure the robe stayed open to exhibit her ample charms through the filmy stuff of the gown underneath. She patted the cushions next to her. When the Earl took a chair instead, pulling it close, she raised one haughty eyebrow.

"You are very cold this day, my Justin. You have not even told me how beautiful I am."

Wrenthe laughed. "Nothing subtle about you, Maringa. Yes, you are magnificently beautiful, as if your mirror didn't tell you. You are as beautiful as . . . 'as the rarest orchid, blooming but once a year at pearly dusk, and I thrice bless'd to see it.' There, was that pretty enough? I caught my brother Stephan writing poems to the housemaid on his last break. No," he said quickly, catching her expression, "I am not poking fun at you, only myself. You know I am no hand at romantical flights."

"You have your moments," she answered with a knowing smile, "but come, would you like some wine?"

"Coffee, if I may." This was no time to have his wits dulled. Maringa rang a little bell on a table next to her—no jumping up for the bell rope every time she wanted something—and the little parlourmaid appeared. While waiting for the tray to be brought, the Earl very casually asked where her new companion was.

"Companion? How did you find out—Oh, you mean the dog!" She laughed nervously, hurrying on when Wrenthe made no comment. "The dog is . . . is in the kitchen, being fed." She was certainly not going to admit she had not even seen the pesky little thing in two days, not after working so hard to get it.

"Did you decide on a name for it yet?" Wrenthe wanted to know, just making nonchalant conversation till his coffee came.

"Of course. I call him . . . Snowball," she decided instantly. White dog, why not? After the bother of convincing her lord that she absolutely required the animal for her happiness, she refused to concede that she'd grown tired of it after showing the thing off once or twice, just as he had predicted. When the girl entered with the tray, Maringa asked her to fetch "dearest Snowball."

"Who, ma'am?"

"The dog, you dolt!"

The maid brought back the pup, who straightaway began to

play with the feathered hem of Maringa's robe, where it was so carefully draped to the floor.

"No, no, precious. You mustn't." Maringa lifted the dog up beside her to make a pretty vignette, but the dog had been shut in the kitchen all day. Not content to sit quietly and look charming, he began to dig in the lace with his front feet, trying to make an escape or get a game going. Instead, as soon as the Earl's attention was diverted to stirring his coffee, the dog was firmly swatted. He yelped in indignation, then sank his needle-sharp milkteeth into the thumb that was holding him so tightly.

"So playful, I just adore puppies," Maringa tittered, her thumb in her mouth, the dog on the floor again, happily savaging a frilly slipper.

The Earl raised his cup to hide his grin. While Maringa was quick to change the topic, speaking of some friends she had met out shopping, Wrenthe dropped a biscuit to the floor, as if by accident. He nudged it with his Hessian-clad foot until the pup was tempted away from the shoe, to sit between Wrenthe's boots and chew something less likely to choke him to death. The Earl excused his own behaviour by remembering that he had undoubtedly paid for the slipper, and certainly for the dog.

Maringa was winding down. How much could a lady have to say, when she hardly ever left the house or saw, supposedly, anyone but his lordship? Conversation was never her strong point, anyway; men would rather be listened to.

"So, my Justin, have you come to tell me about your day? Have you made more speeches in your Parliament?"

"Actually, my dear, I have brought you a gift, a little token of my affection. It's a mere trifle, but I thought you might enjoy it." He handed her the black box, bending to accept her kiss of gratitude.

"Justin, a trifle? It is exquisite! So generous!" She fastened it on her wrist. "It is *magnifico*. . . . It is goodbye?"

That was one thing—another thing—he liked about Maringa: She wasn't born yesterday. When a gentleman made his *chère amie* such an extravagant gesture, it could only mean a graceful parting, as well she knew. The man was relieving his conscience and saying thank you for the good times; the woman was getting something to tide her over, without the cold indignity of a bank draft.

"I am afraid so. You see, I am thinking of settling down. I cannot imagine that the lady I have in mind would accept my paying court to her while I am supporting another woman."

"Then it is only temporary, *caro*. As soon as you are married then *pouf!* I will wait."

He shook his head ruefully. "I hope my marriage will not be like that. If I thought I would desire another woman after my wedding, even one as beautiful as you, then I would never get married."

Maringa had got up to admire her bracelet. Somehow she was behind the Earl, massaging his shoulders, tickling his ear with her whispers.

"If it is that little china doll from the park, she will never satisfy you. You will be bored in a month, with that one. Me, I will wait."

Smiling, the Earl caught her hands and drew her back to her seat. "No, you are wrong about the Incomparable Ferne. I wouldn't be bored; I'd murder her. But come, Mari, your lease is paid until the end of the year, and I am sure you will find another gentleman before the end of the month, if you haven't already." He held his hand up. "No, I am not accusing you. Such an alluring woman as you must have many offers. Maybe you will find someone with nothing to do but take you about. You know you have been complaining at how little time I have for you." When Maringa started to look stormy, he raised one eyebrow. "You are not going to enact me any Cheltenham tragedy, are you? You know the rules. Besides, your heart was never involved."

"How can you say that, Justin? How can you know?" she cried. Of course Maringa knew the rules. Just as certainly did she know she was going to miss this so-generous patron, miss the prestige of being such a man's mistress. Her heart—if she had one—may not be breaking, but her affection for him and his money could not be denied. In fact her affection was growing, in a typically feminine fondness for the one that got away, or was getting away. She threw herself at him, or would have, except for the damn dog caught up in the ruffle of her gown. At Wrenthe's smile, her heartache turned to sheer frustrated greed and prideful indignation that *he* was ending the relationship, not she.

"You—you *bâtard!* You are mean and cruel and I hate you. I hope your proper English lady does accept you, then you'll know what you are missing! And me, I do not wait. I will have a finer gentleman by next week. So there! You go. You get out." She jerked the shaggy dog up from her hems, a patch of feathers and a bit of lace in his mouth, and shoved the pup into the Earl's arms. "And you can take the stupid animal with you," she shouted. "You—"

The Earl's knowledge of Italian was not as extensive as his French, but he got the gist of it. He also noted that in the heat of her passionate outrage Maringa did not lose herself so far as to toss the bracelet back at him. He tucked the dog under one arm, made his most elegant bow and left, smiling like a man whose long shot has just come in first at Ascot.

The tiger could not believe his eyes. His master with a mop?

"No, you looby, it is merely a son of a bitch. Another son of a bitch, if you believe the lady inside. And if you don't shut your mouth you can just return to whatever gutter you sprang from. How are we going to manage the ride home?"

The boy grinned at the idle threat—he'd come from one of his master's own sponsored orphanages—and turned his mind to the problem. He could not drive the phaeton; it needed a lot more muscle to control those chestnuts. The dog would surely fall off the narrow seat if not held, so the tiger volunteered to ride beside the Earl, the dog in his lap, instead of hanging on precariously at the back.

"Very well, brat, though you realise my reputation will be gone."

While the transfer of dog and reins was taking place, however, Snowball decided he had had enough. For all of his ten or so inches, the dog had very definite ideas on the matter. He had been mauled about, kept in the kitchen, smacked and scolded. Now he was secure in the arms of someone who had given him some gentle attention and a sweet, and he was just going to stay there, thank you. He snarled at the hands that reached for him, growling ferociously and ludicrously for such a little scrap of a thing. The Earl and the tiger both laughed. Then the Earl unbuttoned the top two pearl buttons of his waistcoat, nestled the dog in against his lawn shirt, took up the reins, and they were off.

At Grosvenor Square, when Henesley the butler held out his arms to take his lordship's hat, he found his hands full of white fur.

"You'll have to see to it, Henesley, and it doesn't take to rough handling."

"But what *is* it, my lord?"

"Some new-fangled style rug rat, but it's only staying one night. Can you see to my bath?"

Most men of the Earl's standing relied on their valets for constant attendance; not so Wrenthe. He was perfectly capable of shaving himself, selecting his own clothes, putting himself to bed. His valet was in charge of the Earl's wardrobe, of course, and his bedchamber, and helping his master off with his boots and on with the form-moulded jackets. Apart from that, he was dismissed. The Earl could not stand to be fussed over, to have someone hover nearby in breathless anticipation while he tied his neckcloth. All of this was naturally a sore trial to the valet, Jordan, who felt his talents going to waste, even if his employer was always dressed to the nines. He wished to bring the Earl's wavy black hair into a more fashionable Brutus cut; what if it required curling irons? He felt the Earl should wear his shirtpoints as high as any Bond Street beau. If the beaus couldn't turn their heads, well, it was the fashion. Most of all, Jordan felt it was beneath his lordship's dignity to be so capable. With all the snobbishness of a gentleman's gentleman, Jordan felt it was the nobility's right, nay, obligation, to be waited on.

This difference of opinion had lasted almost fifteen years, since Wrenthe had set up an establishment of his own, with neither side conceding a point. Take the Earl's bath, for instance. Jordan felt a valet should make sure the water stayed hot, the towels were warmed, my lord's toes got dried, his robe was held. Wrenthe felt he could manage very well with a few cans of scalding water to add when the tub grew lukewarm, and a towel nearby. He liked to relax in his bath, thinking over his day or his future plans, without any idle conversations about what he would wear later or the temperature of the water. Generally he had succeeded in banishing Jordan from the room while he was actually in the bath, yet the man always appeared, as if by magic, with the brocaded dressing gown the second Wrenthe was out of the tub.

Not so this afternoon. Jordan already had a disapproving look when he announced that the bath was waiting. Word had raced through the servants' quarters of how the master had arrived home, a dog in his waistcoat. After removing the Earl's boots, Jordan waited without saying a word while Wrenthe undressed. Then he picked up the offending waistcoat and the shirt that was under it; holding them at arm's length, he announced he would see to the laundry.

Wrenthe settled back in the lavender-scented water, muscles easing, and felt very satisfied with the day's work. He closed his eyes and, smiling, drew tomorrow-pictures in his head.

When the water cooled off he looked for another can, but there was none. Jordan must have been miffed. He shrugged and got out, taking a towel from the metal warming rack. He had just begun to dry himself when he happened to look down. From the tub to where he stood were wet footprints. Beneath him was a puddle. Yet three feet away, in the middle of his room, where he had not stepped, was another puddle. Two feet beyond that, happily chewing the tassel from one no-longer-shiny Hessian boot, was the infernal dog.

"Jordan!"

The one time the fellow could have been useful was of course the one time he did not answer. The Earl dropped the towel and strode over.

"You, sir, are no gentleman," he shouted. The dog dropped the tassel and whimpered. "You should be ashamed, you ungrateful cur." The dog tried to hide in the carpet. When that failed, the pup simply cowered, trembling. "Well, we all make mistakes, I suppose."

At that the Earl bent to pet the dog, which started thumping its tail against the floor in exuberance at being forgiven, looking up through the white curtain of its hair in adoration. Wrenthe picked it up—most of the dog could fit in one hand—laughing. "No, don't think you can play your tricks off on me, one night is all you are staying. And no more tassels!"

That is what Jordan saw when he returned to hand his master the robe; a tiny white dog being held aloft by a six-foot-plus man who was stark naked. Jordan almost swooned.

Everyone belowstairs, it seemed, had been frantically searching for the creature. The valet was mortified that it should intrude into *his* domain, to disturb the master. That's what came of relaxing in one's duties. Red-faced, he prepared to eliminate the nuisance. To Jordan's further horror, the Earl wished the animal to remain. Jordan thought of giving his notice then and there.

"He found his way up here all by himself, the clever fellow. He deserves to stay. In fact, little friend"—he was addressing the dog, of course, not the sternly disapproving valet who was still rigidly holding the robe—"you are much too smart to be called Snowball. 'Faith, that's a name for kittens. I know, I will call you Diogenes. . . . Jordan, have you ever heard of the philosopher Diogenes?"

A minimal headshake was all he received.

"He's the chap who took his lantern out to find an honest man. Right, Diogenes it will be, for tonight at least. Jordan, I dine at home this evening. Tomorrow you will not only be relieved to see my friend here depart, but you shall also be asked to exert your utmost skill. Tomorrow I call on the Countess."

=== 9 ===
A MAN'S BEST FRIEND

"FINE AS FIVEPENCE, sir, if I do say so myself."

"What? Never tell me you actually approve, Jordan?" the Earl teased, turning this way and that in front of the standing mirror in his bedroom. The outfit was not quite to his taste, which followed Brummell's decrees of understated elegance in sober colours, but in this instance he had taken the valet's advice. The Countess was of another generation, when the men powdered their hair, wore silks and satins and strutted about like peacocks on red high-heeled shoes. She always said the new styles made her sons look like undertakers or solicitors, dashed depressing. As the very presence of the Countess's sons, or daughters, was often depressing enough in her opinion, the Earl had given Jordan a freer rein than usual. As a result he was dressed in a well-fitting burgundy jacket, buff pantaloons, flowered silk waistcoat, cravat tied in the elaborate mathematical, one fob, two seals, his hair done *coup au vent*. If Miss Armstrong had considered him a dandy before, he thought, she should see him now. Actually, if Noelle could see him now she would think, along with most females over the age of fifteen—make that twelve—how vividly the wine-coloured jacket enhanced his dark colouring, how broad his shoulders, how that one curl on his forehead almost pleaded with a woman to brush it aside.

Only Jordan was present, though, and he declared the Earl looked "in prime twig. Much more what we had in mind. Perhaps the ruby stickpin?"

Fop indeed, Wrenthe decided, but all for a good cause. He opened the door to find the puppy looking up at him through a fringe of white hair, black eyes hardly visible, tail waving frantically.

"That . . . that thing has been waiting here since dawn," Jordan reported, sneering. "Kept the housekeeper awake all night; crying to get here, it was."

"Do you know, Diogenes," the Earl said, reaching down to pet the animal, "you have been cutting up a lot of people's rest? I haven't had a moment's peace since I even heard of you! You have me changing the whole pattern of my life, even my clothes." The dog did not seem to care, wagging its whole rear end in excitement. "Yes, yes, I know it is not all your doing, but this has to stop," the Earl continued as he picked the dog up, settling him in the crook of his elbow. Jordan winced.

"I think my pride can stand it," Wrenthe told him as he went down the stairs. "Can yours?"

The Earl of Wrenthe travelled the hour to Surrey in state: the closed carriage with family crest on its panels, liveried driver and groom. He refused outriders, especially for the trip in broad daylight, but as usual carried a loaded pistol in a compartment near the door, just in case. He would much rather have been out in the fresh air on horseback, with a gallop to shake the cobwebs loose. Even if he could have carried the dog, basket and all, though, it certainly would not have been helpful to arrive at his mother's in dusty boots or breeches that smelled of the stable. She would likely have sent him to change, before allowing him in her drawing room in all his dirt. No, much better to be bored and make a good impression, if such were possible, on his much loved but slightly unnatural mother.

The dowager countess of Wrenthe could have been one of the *grandes dames* of the Beau Monde. She had been once, in fact, and still held considerable influence, when she chose to use it. Just as her son had distanced himself from the riotous, wanton Carlton House set without rejecting it, Lady Wrenthe had moved to Surrey. She was close enough to London to remain in close contact with all of her friends and learn all the latest *on dit*'s, yet far enough away from what she considered the frivolous, licentious, degraded atmosphere of the social world. The political sphere she had even less respect for, considering it all rhetoric without even the entertainment value. So she lived nearby in Surrey, rather than at the family's principal seat in Wiltshire, devoting herself to raising prize-winning roses and other people's children. The Countess had established two foundling homes nearby, selecting Surrey so the children could have fresh air to breathe and healthy foods, away from the city's slums, about which even the indomitable Countess could do little. With her last son away at school and her husband dead these many years, she put most of her time and considerable energy into the well-being of her orphans. If her own children felt she cared more for the unfortunate waifs than for them, well, it was just possible.

Empty rattles, that's what she called her own progeny, spoiled care-for-nobodies. It was too soon to tell about Stephan, the youngest, although he was giving every sign of sowing so many wild oats he would have acres to harvest. Most likely trying to live up to his brother Justin's reputation, the Countess supposed. If Stephan ended up half the man, she would be surprised, having a certain fondness for her firstborn. At least Justin had finally developed some sense of responsibility and obligation, after a start that was as witless as it was wild. He had steadied down, maybe a little too indolent, too high on his dignities, but definitely the best of the lot, even with all his moral failings. He was generous, a good landlord; he even tried to do something about reforms in that men's club called Parliament. Handsome devil too, she thought as the butler showed him in.

"How fine you are looking, ma'am," he said, bowing over her hand, then kissing the cheek she offered. "I only hope you are feeling equally as well."

"Hmph," the small white-haired lady replied. "Sit down, sit down. Do you want me to get a crick in my neck? I've forgotten how tall you are."

"Is that a hint that I've been away too long? I would have called sooner if I thought my company would please you."

"Justin. You never call but what it pleases yourself, just like all the rest."

"Nonsense, ma'am. The last time I came you distinctly told me to get back to London where I could—"

"I know what I said, you nodcock." The slightest hint of affection could be detected, if one knew where to look. "So to what do I owe this sign of filial devotion? You must want something, though for the life of me I cannot think what. You don't have one of your by-blows you want me to house in the orphanage, do you?''

''Mother!''

''Well, what then? Stephan only comes to me when he's been sent down again and he's afraid to face you; Corteney only visits when he needs money.''

''Is that fool under the hatches again? I don't understand why he cannot live on his income. You know he's fixed very well,'' the Earl stated with some anger.

''He would live above his income no matter what it was. That harpy he's married to helps him; she thinks nothing but spending every cent she can get her hands on for dresses, parties, jewels . . . I told him to go to you.''

''He'd be wasting his time. I told Corteney I'd pulled him out of River Tick for the last time, that he'd have to manage better or economise. I wasn't going to beggar my estates to settle *his* accounts.'' He smiled. ''I told him to try you.''

''Thank you. At least you don't need money from me, Justin.''

''Come now, Mother. You mustn't think we all have ulterior motives for visiting.'' He coughed slightly, almost as if one of those ulterior motives was caught in his throat. ''What of the girls? Didn't Brynne come to visit a week or two ago?''

''Hah? You wouldn't believe what that clothhead wanted. Quite casually, over tea, your sister asked if perchance I knew a way to prevent a woman's getting pregnant.''

''She's not breeding again! How many does that make?''

''An indecent, immoral number, if you ask me! How they hope to feed that brood, much less educate and settle them all is beyond me. I told her last time that abstinence was the best way I ever heard.''

''So what did you tell her this time?'' Justin wanted to know. ''*Do* you know any ways? I thought ladies never discussed such things.''

''Ladies mightn't. Brynne obviously never did. She's got more hair than wit, anyway. But do you think I would let my girls out of the Home without knowing the facts of life? A daughter's one thing; you marry her off as well as you can and hope for the best. But my girls go out to make a living, with no

94

one to help them and nothing but what they've learned here. I
don't want any of *them* leaving parcels on my doorstep."

"And were you able to help Brynne?"

The countess chuckled. "I told her all right. I also told her
that if I'd known at her age what I know now, neither she nor
the devil's spawn, Stephan, would be around to plague me
now."

They both laughed, then the Earl stood up. "Well, you are
wrong," he told her, going to the door. "I have come solely for
the purpose of bringing you a present." He left for a moment,
returning with a straw picnic hamper, its lid slightly open.

"Lunch, Justin? You know we could have fed you. . . . I only
plead poverty for Corteney's sake."

"Don't be absurd, Mother. It's a very special gift." He set
the basket down by his chair, lifted out the puppy, which
yawned, showing a pink tongue, and sat by the Earl's boot,
blinking.

The Countess raised her lorgnette on its black ribbon. She
looked through it at the dog, then at the Earl. Then at the dog
again.

"Indeed," was all she said, although she could not have been
more surprised if the Staffordshire dogs on her mantel had
barked at her.

"It's a very rare breed, a Maltese, it's called," the Earl said
hurriedly, "They are getting to be all the crack in London. I
brought it for you because I thought you might be lonely, with
Stephan spending his holidays in Town now, and the girls so
busy. I mean, I know you're awfully involved with the Homes,
but while you are here, the little chap could sit nearby and be a
. . . a companion."

The Countess said nothing. She did not have to. They both
knew there were two spinster relations somewhere about the
place, grey mousy females who were being paid, by way of
giving them a living, for acting as Lady Wrenthe's companions.
As for Stephan, his mother had sworn he'd be the death of her,
and she had forbidden him the Surrey house. Justin might be
up to his brother's fits and starts; she was too old for schoolboy
pranks.

The Earl bent forward to rub the dog's ears, and keep him

from chewing the cabriole leg chair. Pressing gamely onward, he declared, "He is very clever for a dog. Not like those hounds I used to keep." (Which were never permitted in the house, he recalled, somewhat too late.) "His father's name was Plato. I've been calling him Diogenes."

At his mother's sceptical look and another "Indeed," he had the grace to look a little embarrassed. "He keeps finding my bedroom door, that's all."

"Perhaps you should keep him then," the Countess said, watching her very large son fondle a very small dog. This was more amusing than teasing poor Brynne. "You two seem to have an affinity for each other."

"No, I, ah, know where I could get another. This one's just for you." To prove it, he hoisted the pup and sat him in the Countess's taupe satin lap. Then, because he had not grown to be thirty-five years old without learning something of this stone-hearted mother of his, he added, "He's been abused, you see. The last owner beat him and neglected him. You can see where I had to remove the tyke to a better home."

Two thin arms instantly folded around the dog protectively. "Someone hurt this . . . this sweet little thing?" She could not believe it. "Poor baby," she crooned, "no one will ever hurt you again." The dog rolled over to have his chest scratched by one diamond-ringed finger.

The mutt must have listened to the lecture in the carriage, the Earl thought, relieved. Wrenthe had looked Diogenes straight in the eye, as straight as he could with something trying to grab the end of his cravat, and told the dog he would be hung out to dry if he growled, snapped or in any way disgraced himself. So far so good, but there was still some heavy sailing ahead. Wrenthe cleared his throat.

"I'm certain you'll want to meet the two young women who raised the dog," he began.

"You are?" she asked, delighted to see him squirm.

"Of course. They know all about the breed. It's quite ancient, you know. They can even spout Latin about it. You will want to know what Diogenes here eats, how to take care of his coat, et cetera."

"I will?" spoken unhelpfully by one who knew all of the

London gossip, although she would never let on to this jackanapes trying to put one over on her. His collar must have shrunk a bit in the day's heat, the way he pulled on it.

"Yes, they are quite charming young women. Do you remember Sterling? Armstrong, he was, the Ambassador? These are his children."

"That old reprobate? At least he added a little colour to the Foreign Bureau. His wife passed on too, I believe, a quiet, retiring girl. A real mismatch, if I remember. She was a Wycombe, wasn't she? Related to that awful woman who died in some heathen country I never heard of. I don't think I'd care to know any children from that marriage." The Countess was going to play the game to its fullest.

"Oh no, they're perfectly respectable, very well behaved," he lied. "The younger is a diamond of the first water, and you would admire the older. She's very big on education for the lower classes, very well read, too."

"But I am very busy," Lady Wrenthe complained, waving one hand vaguely to encompass her whole world, which she was ready to dump in a moment, to meet the young women, or woman, responsible for this interesting development. Why, the boy looked to be shaping up at last. The dowager had flinched every time she'd thought of the estates going to Corteney or his sons. Now here was Justin putting himself out for a marriageable female, wanting his mother to meet her. She had thought she'd not live to see the day. And what a delightful challenge, to figure out which sister had caught his fancy, after all these years. From what she'd heard, the beauty hadn't much substance, and the older had countenance. Would Justin choose a young miss who might be biddable or a moderately attractive one with a degree of conversation? She couldn't wait. ". . . Much too busy to entertain, you know?"

"It wouldn't have to be anything much, Mother. I thought I might bring the ladies and their aunt out for tea one afternoon. Unless you wished to come to Town to do some shopping or whatever? We could make up a party for the Theatre, nothing formal, you understand, just to talk about the dog, of course."

"Of course," his mother agreed, smiling. "And I truly

97

would like to accommodate you, dearest. However"—her smile grew-"I'm frightfully involved in raising money for the new wing to the Boys' School. Once that's all done, I am sure I could manage something."

Wrenthe smiled, too. Then he grinned and laughed out loud. "Touché, Mama. How much?"

As the Earl left his mother, before the door was closed, he could hear her talking to the dog still on her lap. He did not doubt for an instant that he was meant to hear every word.

"Well, now my companions will have something to keep them busy, Diogenes, caring for you. And isn't it wonderful how my son Justin comes to visit, bringing me gifts, without wanting anything at all!"

═10═

SURREY TEA

A FEW DAYS later the Earl's carriage was again en route to Surrey. This time Wrenthe had the three Armstrong ladies for company, no dogs. His mother's invitation to tea had been for 2:00, so the Earl had told the ladies he would fetch them at 12:30. Having experience with Ferne and many another female, he allowed an extra half hour for the women to keep him waiting, rather than arrive late in Surrey, since nothing set his mother off so much as tardiness. It showed a want of consideration towards others, she considered, and a lack of personal discipline. The Earl was determined to give this visit every best chance. He was surprised, then, when all three of the ladies were ready at his arrival. Although Ferne's lip trembled and Noelle's eyes looked stormy, it was simply a matter of buttoning pelisses and tying bonnets before they were off.

The Earl could not have any private conversation with Noelle, simply complimenting each woman in turn—indeed they all looked superb—before he very properly offered his arm to Aunt Hattie to escort her to the carriage. Once he had all the ladies inside, however, he had to tell his coachman, in a low voice, to take the trip particularly slowly, no springing the team, no shortcuts. Devilish tricky business, he thought, this social politicking. No wonder he preferred the House of Lords.

Things were not much easier in the Countess's elegant drawing room. All of the ladies were impressed by the size and magnificence of Lady Wrenthe's home. They drove up an elm-shaded carriageway, past a lake with a small pavilion on its island, a formal topiary garden, a maze, then the rose gardens, before even seeing the house itself. Except that it was no house; it was a Palladian mansion, with Greek colonnades, this

99

"minor" property of the Wrenthor holdings. Sterlingwood in Derbyshire would have fit on the covered portico! Ferne especially seemed awed at the grandeur, intimidated by the one small woman who ruled here. After her polite curtsey and whispered thank-you-for-the-invitation, she sat quietly, not really taking part in the conversation, while the Countess was enthusing over her new pet with surprising sincerity. This was not what Lord Wrenthe had in mind, so he kept trying to draw Ferne out. His mother would certainly not be interested in any tongue-tied chit. When the others were done complimenting his mother's house and seeking mutual acquaintances, he asked Ferne to tell the Countess about the Maltese breed. Looking downward, she referred him to Noelle as the expert.

Dutifully Noelle briefly related the history as it was known, then the particular background of the dog Lady Wrenthe had adopted. Aunt Hattie added some helpful clues as to keeping its coat soft and white, but Ferne said little, answering the Earl's leading questions with only a murmured word or two.

The Countess, for once keeping a check on her ascerbic tongue, to her son's amazement, seemed to understand his mission and came to the rescue: "I understand the dog's previous owner was unsuitable, Miss Ferne, is that correct?"

"Noelle certainly thought so, my lady," Ferne assured her naively. "She said I was never ever to mention Miss Polieri again, and there you did, right off. See, Nellie?" Ferne clasped her hand over her mouth when she saw the others' looks of dismay. "Oh! I thought you meant—"

The Countess laughed, delighted to see her son blush. Must be the first time in ten years, she thought. What a merry dance the little peagoose would lead him, yet that seemed to be his preference, with all the attention he'd been trying to focus on her. It seemed a shame. The older gal had a great deal of presence, picking up the conversation neatly, explaining how the previous owner had not lived up to their contract, just as if the sister hadn't made a slip, just as if the Countess didn't know the identity of her son's mistress. Yes, here was a female worthy of a Wrenthe. Couldn't hold a candle to the other for looks, of course, but the Countess would have thought Justin beyond all that. Once again she wondered how all of her children could be so bacon-brained.

Either way, the Countess was determined to further this courtship. After tea with the spinster relations, who listened avidly to directions for grooming the creature they already doted on, the Countess suggested that her son escort Ferne through the rose gardens. She thought Noelle might wish to go on a brief tour of the Girls' Home, since Miss Armstrong had expressed interest. Aunt Hattie felt she would rather rest quietly, after such a lavish tea. The Earl approved this plan, which would show his mother Noelle's serious, caring nature, at the same time removing her paper-skulled sister from the Countess's vicinity, before Ferne bungled the whole affair with her artless prattle. His ready acquiescence, however, only confirmed to both Noelle and Lady Wrenthe that he welcomed the opportunity to spend time privately with Ferne, relatively unchaperoned.

Lady Wrenthe saw a quick look of pain cross Noelle's face, which she interpreted as fear for her sister's reputation. To reassure her young guest, the Countess made sure the companions took Diogenes out to the garden also, for some exercise, but she was determined to give Justin time to woo his pretty nitwit.

Whatever emotions were battling within Noelle, she forgot them as she viewed the Girls' Home. This was like no orphanage she had ever heard of, or had nightmarish visions of in her worst dreams. What if they hadn't had Sterlingwood or Aunt Hattie? She'd pictured her brother and sister in some vile workhouse, dressed in tatters, racked by coughs, plagued by vermin. Or in a factory or a mine. A chill went through her. Yet here were rooms full of laughing, scrubbed little girls in neat grey dresses with white pinafores, their hair all in braids with plaid ribbons. Some sat at desks learning their letters, while others chattered over their needlework. A cooking lesson must have been going on in the kitchen, for six flour-covered moppets were kneading dough, while in the nursery three older girls watched over the infants. Everything was clean and orderly; all the girls smiled and bobbed their curtseys. Noelle was overwhelmed and listened avidly to the Countess's plans and theories, which the white-haired dowager was happy to relate. While Noelle might care a great deal about raising dogs, the Countess's hobbyhorse was her children. Not the twiddle-poops she birthed, she stated in disgust, they'd had every advantage in the world. These children, with nothing, sometimes not even a name, *these* children needed her.

There was no question but that Noelle would vow to do everything she could to help. She only wished her finances permitted her to be as generous as she wanted. She felt guilty, spending so much on gowns and fripperies, while these children had so little.

It was hard to put into words without sounding mean-spirited, but her hostess understood perfectly. Patting Noelle's arm, she said, "Gammon, child, you deserve some pleasures, too. And you have to have all that fancy trapping to live in Society. It's absurd, but that's the way it is, and you have to do it, once at least. Besides, there are other ways you can help."

Before Noelle realized it, she'd hired another servant, a young girl named Janie to be an assistant ladies' maid, so she might learn and gain references for an honest, professional future. Noelle's resources could surely cover such an expense and, as Lady Wrenthe explained, her eyes twinkling, if the Armstrongs were going to make a splash, there would be ample work combing, curling, pressing, trimming, buttoning, for at least three abigails.

Furthermore, as she continued on the return to the house, she was thinking of adding a new wing, which would require a great deal of money. If she went to London to seek pledges from her friends and acquaintances, Noelle could help with that, too.

"I could, ma'am?" Noelle was dubious. "I know almost no one, certainly no one with any amount of money."

"No, no, I know all those people. I cannot simply walk up to Lord Wolfe, though, for example, and ask for money before he loses it at the tables. It takes more subtlety. But what if I were in Town to introduce two young ladies around? I'd have an excuse to be at all those parties everyone knows I detest, and I could just casually mention the new wing."

"You . . . you would do that for us?"

"Stuff and nonsense, girl," the Countess said gruffly. "I wouldn't be doing it for you. I'd be doing it for my children."

Aunt Hattie was sitting with her ever-present workbasket. When Noelle described the Countess's labours with such enthusiasm, repeating her promise to lend any aid she could, her aunt declared that she could help also. Holding up her knitting, she told an amused audience that if she could make doggie coats she could surely make hats and mittens and socks, and write her friends in Bath to help, too! She was never one to believe a lady had to keep to purely decorative needlework, she told the Countess, setting her spectacles firmly in place again. After all, how many seat coverings could anyone use? If people looked down their noses at her, at least she'd have the satisfaction of knowing someone would be warmer for her efforts. Lady Wrenthe swore quite fondly that no one would dare sneer at such honest labor, not while *she* was in Town.

"Oh, are you going to London, Mother?" asked her son, coming in through the French doors with Ferne.

"I am going to have to, to raise funds, in spite of your generosity. Miss Noelle has offered her help, and I am sure I can count on Miss Ferne to attract would-be benefactors." This last was said to get a rise from Wrenthe, but he just smiled in agreement. Was it that he didn't care enough to be jealous, the Countess wondered, or too sure of himself? And here she thought she'd guessed it. Maybe there was hope to switch his affections after all.

The Countess would not have been so complacent if she had looked beyond Aunt Hattie and past the open doors to the scene in the rose garden. Noelle had, and the picture stayed with her. Much later, when she was alone, sitting up in her bed with only one candle left burning, the whole household asleep, she remembered the incredible afternoon. The tiny Countess, who looked like a gust of wind would blow her away, yet who had ideas and opinions as unshakeable as a brick tavern, had reached up to kiss Noelle goodbye, to everyone's surprise, and promised to be in London before a se'nnight passed. The Armstrongs were finally going to have a sponsor! And then that ride home, with the Earl at his most charming, laughing and joking with Ferne, teasing Aunt Hattie. Dinner, and telling Win about the wonderful work Lady Wrenthe was doing. And through it all, just behind her eyes, Noelle kept seeing the Earl and Ferne in the rose garden.

They had been sitting on a stone bench, watching Diogenes's antics as he tried to catch a butterfly. Ferne clapped her hands in delight and the Earl laughed his rich, warm laugh. They looked so happy, so at ease in each other's company. And so attractive, Ferne's fairness against the Earl's dark, tanned skin. He'd taken her hand to raise her from the bench, yet did not let go immediately.

Noelle thought she would see that picture forever. She got out of bed and took up the candle. Barefoot and in her lawn nightgown that left nothing showing but her pale face, auburn curls and big green eyes, she padded over to stare at Aunt Sylvia's portrait. It was of a young Sylvia Wycombe, perhaps close to Noelle's age, wearing a blue gown and smiling.

"Is that what happened to you?" Noelle asked the lady in the portrait. "Did you once have a dream, too?"

A tear trickled down her cheek.

=== 11 ===
THE DERBY ROSEBUD

THE COUNTESS DESCENDED on her son's Grosvenor Square mansion like visiting royalty. She rode in the first carriage with her lady's maid and her secretary. The companions came next, with Diogenes, who deserted them immediately for the Earl, then two baggage carts filled with clothing, household items the Countess could not live without and fruits from her own succession houses. When the Earl dared to make note of all this, his mother recommended he take rooms at the Clarendon Hotel, or go visit one of his holdings. Laughing, he vowed he would not miss this for the world, and escaped to his study, followed by a tiny white shadow, to his mother's amusement. She proceeded to reclaim a suite of rooms, to move furniture in the reception rooms, to banish pieces she'd hated when she lived there, and in general turn the previously well-run if austere bachelor establishment topsy-turvy. Only the Earl's study was left untouched, on dire threats. His bedroom—even his bedroom, by Jupiter!—was tampered with, with fresh hangings for the bed, a new coat of beeswax on the dark furniture and a straw basket on the floor. Jordan was only prevented from immediately handing in his notice by a strong appeal to his sense of loyalty. After two days of this the Earl abandoned poor James Waverly, who had always been terrified of his small, domineering aunt, and went to his clubs. It was noticed, however, that on his way past the newly filled urn on the hall table, he did select a flower for his buttonhole.

The Countess decided to make her reentry into Society at the Drury Lane Theatre, where the great Kean was doing Othello. Everyone would be there and, for once, paying attention to the stage. Intermissions were something else. The Earl's box was so filled with feathered headpieces it looked like an aviary. Some of the women were simply happy to see their old friend; some were curious as to the connection between the Wrenthes and those hurly-burly Armstrongs; still others, those with eligible daughters, wanted to corner the elusive Earl and the handsome young Viscount. The Earl put his arm on Win's shoulder and propelled him from the box, claiming they were going to fetch refreshments for the ladies.

Out in the hall, away from the crush, Winston exhaled in relief. Grinning, Wrenthe told him, "Be glad you've only got looks and a title. If you were rich besides, they'd have you drawn and quartered before dawn!"

Win laughingly asked how the Earl had managed to avoid the man-traps for so long.

"Well, after a while the hunters give it up as hopeless and go after new blood. Let the wily old fox give you some tips, cub. One, never pay particular attention to any one lady. Don't even join some belle's court. First thing you know she's singled you out and her papa's shaking your hand. Second, don't . . ."

They moved on down the hall.

The Countess was enjoying herself immensely. Kean was good, but, oh, the play in her box! Salley Jersey, Emily Cowper, even Lady Bedford were introduced to the Armstrongs, children of her dear friends, Viscount and Lady Sterling, sadly departed . . . didn't Sally remember that sweet Felice Wycombe? Yes, that was the Viscount who just left with Wrenthe, a charming boy, very devoted to his lands. Didn't Emily think he'd break his share of hearts? Of course she was still carrying on with her charitable work, even bigger projects now that dear Noelle was going to assist her; even Mrs. Hattie Deighton was going to help, such a generosity of spirit.

Lady Wrenthe was almost disappointed, it was so easy. The girls had created enough of a stir on their own, looking as pretty as pictures, without any of her finagling, yet in two shakes, they were accepted, quite a different thing. It was nothing to deliberate over the invitation to Lady Trippe's ball, as though considering if her protégées could get along without her; the invitation was immediately extended to all of the ladies. A day's outing to Richmond? How delightful, and she wondered if her young friends had seen it yet. So it went. Noelle had nothing to do but smile and curtsey and sit bemused while their futures were plotted for them.

At the second intermission, the box was inundated with black evening coats instead of feathers and furbelows. The gentlemen all wanted to be presented to the ladies, now that they were given the nod. In fact, the Armstrongs bid fair to becoming this Season's belles, and to exclaim over Ferne's beauty and Noelle's grace was quickly becoming the fashion. Anyone with any pretensions to being au courant had to make their acquaintance. Ferne was too moved by Kean's dramatic performance to care about all the attention, though she blushed adorably at some of the outlandish compliments, which only raised her stock in some eyes. She was not so embarrassed by the ogling from the audience this time either. Perhaps this crowd was better behaved than the one at the Opera because they were subdued, like Ferne, by the power of England's greatest actor. Perhaps they were not staring so rudely, scrutinizing the ladies like so much furniture, because the Armstrongs now shared the box of the Countess of Wrenthe, one of the Beau Monde's favorite eccentrics.

At the last curtain Ferne was weeping into Winston's handkerchief, to his disgust, and Noelle's eyes were shiny with moisture. The Countess declared herself very pleased with the night's performance. She only smiled when her son placed her shawl over her shoulders and quietly asked which performance she was referring to, the great Kean's or her own.

"You'll be disappointed, girl, it's nothing so wonderful," the Countess warned Noelle as they waited for their carriage to approach the covered walk.

"I know, Mama used to tell me, stale sandwiches, petty restrictions, bad lighting and indifferent music. But it's Almack's! Whatever else happens, we got to Almack's."

Noelle's gamble had paid off, and she was exhilarated with her success. Even Ferne was glowing in anticipation of her first real dance. With the confidence born of the Earl's admiration and the Countess's predictions, she was radiant. Dressed in white, as befitted a debutante, she had a vibrancy missing in the other young girls. Her gown was classically simple, gathered under the bust in a pink ribbon sash, which held a nosegay of pink rosebuds. The hem was trimmed with the same ribbon and a rose or two, and one pink satin slipper tapped the floor, waiting for Winston to lead her out for the first dance. Her golden hair was piled on top of her head, held with a tiara of the same pink flowers, with one long blond ringlet falling to her shoulder. Her blue eyes sparkled in delight at just being there. Almost every eye in the room noticed the handsome, fair couple.

The Earl himself was to lead Noelle out for the first cotillion, on his mother's directions, since Noelle was the older sister. Nell wished it was not so; being her partner's second choice, as she thought, was lowering. Yet the compliment was so obvious in his dark eyes, the rare smile of his seemed to tell her she was the most beautiful girl in the room. Even if it wasn't close to the truth, she could enjoy the dance and her partner, who to her was certainly the most attractive man there. Noelle's own gown was one of Madame Franchot's, and she felt elegant in it. A deep pink satin with an overdress of white Valenciennes lace, it was no debutante's party frock. Cut low, draped superbly, it showed her appealing figure to every advantage, without the least hint of fastness. That so-white skin gleamed under the Titian curls, except where the slighest dusting of powder hid the dratted freckles. Many eyes followed Noelle too, and not just because she was dancing with one of England's most eligible bachelors.

Noelle and Ferne switched partners for the second set, a country dance, and all along the walls where the bachelors stood, in the gilded chairs where the chaperones kept watch, in little knots of giddy misses, people again took note. Here was the Earl of Wrenthe, at Almack's for the first time in memory, dancing with a debutante! Was he caught at last, or just doing the pretty for his mother's friends? What a delicious bit of gossip, either way!

And either way, the girls were suddenly accredited beauties.

The distinguished patronage, the Earl's particularities, their own entrancing freshness, drew a crowd to where the Countess stood, all waiting to be introduced at the end of the dance.

There were smooth-faced lads, ready to take advantage of their recent acquaintance with Win, a scattering of uniforms, cronies of Wrenthe's from his clubs and the House, men closer to his mother's age. There were also some women with daughters in hand, matchmaking motives in heart, offering the Misses Armstrong friendship of their own sex. The Countess was a conductor, waving a baton at the orchestra, a particularly inept group, judging from the glance she privately sent her son. He showed his true statesmanship by smiling affably at everyone, then retreating. He paused by Aunt Hattie's nearby seat, where she was almost nodding off.

"My mother is ample chaperone, Mrs. Deighton, so there is no need for us all to be bored. Perhaps you would care to join me in the card room?" He was unprepared for the way those myopic eyes lighted up, so he hurriedly added, "It's only chicken stakes, ma'am, ha'penny points, you know."

"Oh, that's no matter. I can't tell you how delighted I would be, my lord." She was fumbling in her reticule for her spectacles. "Ah, here they are. Couldn't see the cards without them. As I was saying, it's been years since I've had a decent game; the children don't like to play with me."

As the Earl started to lead Aunt Hattie from the room, a hand on his arm and a pleading look from Winston had to be laughingly rebuffed.

"Sorry, old man, someone has to stay and guard the ladies."

In revenge, Win taunted back: "In that case I won't warn you about Aunt Hattie."

It was with some trepidation, therefore, that the Earl seated Mrs. Deighton at a whist table, making introductions. Good grief, he thought, what now from the Armstrongs? And here he'd decided anything would be more peaceful than seeing those glorious green eyes laugh up at Ferddie Millbrooke. And if he had to watch that oily Lieutenant Ramsey put his arm where the Earl wished his to be, he'd most likely call the man out. This had to stop. But what if the aunt cheated at cards? He took a stance behind her chair . . . and watched in astonishment as the plump little grey-haired lady adjusted her spectacles, and proceeded to make the cards sing through her fingers with all the expertise of a Downe Street dealer.

Ferne did not notice the Earl's absence, but Noelle did. She knew his good manners would prevent him from asking Ferne to dance more than twice during the evening or from drawing attention to her by hanging about, yet he did not seek out any other partners. This seemed to prove his *tendre* for Ferne, if Noelle needed any further evidence. She laughed a little harder at Lord Millbrooke's wit, putting the Earl from her mind. Except that the Lieutenant did not have as broad a chest as Wrenthe, the handsome scarlet regimentals notwithstanding; Mr. Harcourt's leg was not as well muscled in his knee breeches and silk stockings; the Marquis of Cheyne was not as graceful on the dance floor, etc., etc.

Ferne was making no such comparisons. In her delightful way she was enjoying each new partner offered to her, while each gentleman's charm blossomed under such a light. When it was seen that overly fulsome compliments, as were the style, only made Miss Ferne blush and look downwards, denying her partner the sight of those heavenly blue eyes, the men relaxed even more. Ferne was pleased, actually interested, to listen to stories of their horses and dogs and rural properties and brothers and sisters . . . and whatever *real* people talked of, when they were not busy with all the flummery of courtship. Miss Ferne was no coquette, it was unanimously decided; she was adorable and *nice*. What a relief, especially to Winnie's sporting friends. They were here under duress anyway, but what a change, dancing with a pretty girl and actually enjoying it! She didn't even chide a fellow for missing a step or two. Perhaps there was something to this marriage mart business after all.

At the orchestra's intermission, Ferne was at the centre of a group of young people of both sexes, all laughing and making plans to meet at Lady Trippe's ball, for rides in the park, perhaps a picnic if the weather held. When the music began again it was Ferne, not the lady patronesses, who sorted out all of her new friends, making sure all of the girls had partners. This naturally endeared her to all of the girls and all of their mamas, to everyone, in fact, but Winston, whose partners tended to have spots or two left feet or fits of the giggles. He could only have recourse to what Nell had quoted their father as saying: "When the girl can't dance, isn't pretty and has no conversation, make the best of it. Pretend she's going to marry your worst enemy. Better yet, plan to introduce 'em." Winston was always able to smile at the girls and thank them sincerely for the dance.

Noelle had spent the break period in conversation with a retired Admiral who had known her father, an undersecretary in the War Department and two military gentlemen, discussing the news from the Peninsula. She hardly noticed the music begin, so engrossed was she, until the Captain recalled he was to partner her. He declared that he hated to deprive the others of such an informed listener, but he had been waiting all evening for the dance.

After that Noelle's partner was a Viscount, then she sat out with a gouty old gentleman who said he had recognized her for a Wycombe. Hoping for information, Noelle eagerly asked if he had known Aunt Sylvia well but he answered, laughing, that he'd sooner have hugged a bear. Before he could say why, he was shushed by a pretty young woman who turned out to be his married daughter, fearing for Noelle's sensibilities. Assuring them that she had none, Noelle asked if she might call on Lady Brock and her father, when he might be permitted to tell the story. Glancing over her shoulder, Noelle saw Wrenthe dancing with Ferne. She quickly turned back to the conversation.

A few dances later—she could not help noticing that the Earl danced with Sally Jersey, then one of the officers' wives—a waltz was played. Noelle made sure that Ferne was safely sipping a lemonade, since it was not permitted for any young lady to dance the waltz without approval from one of the patronesses. The new German dance was considered too fast, unsuitable for the younger set as it was too conducive to taking liberties. It was with considerable surprise, therefore, that Noelle saw Lady Jersey approaching, the Earl at her side. Sally gave her smiling nod, pleased to give the gathering more to gossip over.

Noelle had nothing to say. Her very first waltz ever, if you didn't count Win or the dancing master, and in the arms of the one man present tonight who made her knees quiver. If this was to be her life's portion of magic, she'd enjoy it to the fullest. She closed her eyes and relaxed in his hold, content to let the music and his nearness flow through her.

Contrary to his desires, which were to draw Miss Armstrong even closer and kiss each blue-veined eyelid, for a start, the Earl asked how she was enjoying her evening.

"Wonderfully, my lord." She was still floating.

"And was it everything you expected?"

"Yes, it was. I'm sure you're thinking that it is all shallow and these people should be home caring for their tenants, or whatever. But tonight I refuse to argue, even with you." When she saw one of those heavy eyebrows raise she went on: "I don't want to hear any cynical remarks. See how happy Ferne is, all the people she's met? Everyone has been so nice to us, so kind. We've made friends, I hope, and had reasonable conversations. Who do you think we could talk to at home, the pigs? I can never thank your mother enough for what she did for us."

"No need, she's quite pleased herself. Nearly everyone who waits for an introduction between dances gets treated to a description of her latest project. She's got a lot of pledges already. Most of the patronesses have promised her cheques also. They had to, after she livened up their dull gathering for them."

"Hmm?"

"The Armstrong women! Don't you realize what successes you are? Mother has had nothing but compliments all night. Already Ferne is being called the Derby Rosebud."

Noelle smiled proudly. The Earl didn't say that she herself was being lauded as a true original, nor that he was thinking how, in her white lace, she reminded him of a rose in the snow, exquisite, brave, vulnerable. He shook himself in his own mind. It was this bewitching minx and the waltz, he cautioned. It would pass.

"Taylor will be pleased, too."

Shaken from his own thoughts, his turn to be almost lost in the music and the moment, the Earl had to ask Noelle to repeat herself.

"Taylor will be pleased, too, I said. He bet half a year's wages on our getting to Almack's." She smiled. "I aim to see he donates some of that to your mother's children."

"Speaking of bets, Miss Noelle, did you know that your aunt is a remarkable card player? She has just relieved half the dowagers of their pocket money."

"No, is she?" Noelle replied with a particularly dainty giggle. "I suspected as much. We always hated playing with her . . . she never let us win! I'll have to tell Winston. He has been afraid to gamble with his new friends, figuring that if Aunt Hattie could beat him, he had no business playing."

The Earl joined her in laughter as the dance ended. "You can safely tell him that if he comes close to her in skill, his fortune is made."

Somehow, when they walked off the floor, the Earl forgot to remove his hand from Noelle's waist, until they were almost at the Countess's side. The warm spot where it had been grew cold, matching the place in Noelle's heart, but she'd had her night at Almack's!

=12=

CLOUDS

AS THE LONDON Season reached its height, so did the Armstrongs' popularity. The Chauncey Square house was often full of young men with floral offerings, or young women with fashion magazines or older ladies with workbaskets. At other times the house was empty, each member going his or her own way, meeting only at breakfast to discuss which invitations to accept, or in the carriage riding to some function. At the dances, routs, suppers, they each had their own circles. As at Lady Trippe's ball, the Countess established her coterie of the most affluent, while Aunt Hattie immediately headed for the card room, set aside for those not wishing to dance. Ferne was instantly beseiged by her admirers, all clamouring for a place on her dance card. Many were wearing new waistcoats embroidered with rosebuds, and one enterprising cavalier had fernlike tracery embroidered on his white satin, which he vowed to wear until Ferne was his. She spent the intermissions with a merry knot of other debutantes and their beaus; she danced every dance, one with the Earl, to the envy of all her new female friends, and occasionally with older men. It was with the younger set that she was easiest, however, and when Noelle could most often hear her soft laughter.

Noelle found herself with her own admirers: military men who liked to talk of their exploits, some of the older men about Town who liked being seen with the new rage, and some seriously interested—and interesting—gentlemen. She also deepened her friendship with Lady Brock, who in turn introduced her to other pleasant women. Noelle found the evening less exciting than the night at Almack's, waiting for that official acceptance, but she was still enjoying herself. Until, that is, the dance she was supposed to have with Justin Wrenthe.

The Earl had requested her hand for an earlier set, and Noelle felt a very distinct satisfaction in telling him she was already promised to the Marquis of Cheyne. Wrenthe nodded pleasantly and requested a later dance, after the intermission, perhaps. Noelle had agreed, then pattered off in her satin slippers, the peach satin of her new gown swirling about her hips. The Earl had stood watching, that same public smile fixed in place, but those closest could see his jaws clenching it in position. He stood a while longer before joining a group of gentlemen discussing politics in one of Lady Trippe's side rooms. When he returned later, Noelle was just concluding a fast-paced waltz with Lieutenant Ramsey. Breathless, she merely laughed when the Lieutenant bowed and kissed her hand. Fluttering her fan, she turned to Wrenthe.

With so many eyes on them as they stood at the edge of the dance floor, the Earl continued to smile, but his low-spoken words were anything but polite: "Madam, you are turning into a flirt. First the nobility, then the militia. I might have expected as much from your sister, with her ramshackle notions of respectability, but I thought you had more sense. I see I was mistaken. You are merely collecting hearts for your scrapbook."

Noelle was stunned. She couldn't see where she'd done anything beyond enjoy herself. Furthermore, although the Earl had certainly been a big help in getting them established, no one had given him the right to take her to task. Of all the insufferable, conceited—No, she would not lose her temper, not in front of Lady Trippe's hundred guests, most of whom were watching the Earl, as usual, for any new *on dit*'s. Her pointed little chin thrust upwards, Noelle said in her sweetest voice, "I am sorry I will not be able to have this dance with you, my lord. I seem to have torn a flounce and must go repair it." With that she gave a *very* low curtsey and walked from the room. Unfortunately, her sweetest voice was not her softest, since all of those waiting nearby for the music to start had also heard her. They also noticed, quite easily, that there was not a single flounce, ruffle or ribbon on Miss Armstrong's gown.

What the gossips made of that was anybody's guess. The Earl

requested a dance with a pasty-faced girl in white tulle, a long-in-the-tooth drab from the sidelines. The betting book at White's would see a lot of new entries before dawn. The Earl knew the ways of the social world, knew that his every move was discussed, just because he was Wrenthe, and for so long totally unsocial, totally discreet. Now here he was, making a cake of himself in public, causing scenes like the veriest nimwit. He berated himself for every kind of fool, but feared he would only do it again.

Noelle, meanwhile, wished to go home, but it would look too peculiar, and she was promised for the next dances. She thought she might find Win to take her outside for some fresh air—Lord knew it was stuffy enough here—but her brother was nowhere to be seen. He'd done his duty dances with Miss Isabella Trippe, various of Ferne's friends, a few of the unfortunates on the sidelines, then disappeared, into the card room, most likely. He had discovered that, while he did not have Aunt Hattie's near infallibility, he did have some skill with the cards, and was acquiring a taste for the play. Noelle did not think he'd go too deep, not when he knew so well how much a new bull cost, how many men he would have to hire for harvesting. More worrisome to Noelle was the taste for champagne Win was also acquiring, and which was flowing freely at the ball, but she was not going to worry about it now. Now she wanted only to be away from here. She walked towards the balcony until she realized how it would look, if people wanted to think the worst of her. So she just stood in the doorway, letting the breeze cool her cheeks. Who cared if *he* thought she was meeting a man there anyway? That miserable, obnoxious beast! How could he have said that to her? Besides her own confusion—one minute he was kindness itself, the next vicious—she could not figure why the Earl was so well thought of. Was she the only one he was rude to, ill-tempered and irascible with? And here she was worrying that she was forming a partiality for the man. Well, not anymore! She didn't even know if she wanted him to marry Ferne now.

It took a great deal of fortitude, and a quick sip of champagne, to walk back into the ballroom past all the staring tabbies to find her next partner.

*   *   *

At Maria Sefton's rout party the Earl apologised, choking a little on the words, making a garbled excuse of his mother's protection, modern morals, an excess of wine—anything but the truth, that he had been torn ragged by jealousy. Noelle accepted the apology in the spirit in which it was given, grudgingly, but the two did not return immediately to their former understanding. Noelle was distrustful and, in spite of herself, censoring her behaviour for his approval. For his part, the Earl was having to exert too much control over his emotions to relax in her presence. At least they did not give the *ton* anything more to talk about, acting cordially when they met at all the functions.

As the Season wore on people no longer remarked that Lord Wrenthe invariably danced with both sisters at the parties, yet seemed to treat Ferne with less formality. He called at Chauncey Square, took Miss Ferne out driving, but could not be considered part of her court. Everyone waited. The last great ball of the Season was approaching, the Countess of Wrenthe's own gala, ostensibly to dedicate the new wing she was planning for her children's homes. In effect, it was her final fund-raising project. Since this was to be the last major function, and at Wrenthe House, which was infrequently open to company, and since she was Lady Wrenthe, nearly everyone invited sent in an acceptance. No one could be so dense as to come without a cheque for the orphanage. It was expected, and eagerly anticipated, that the Earl would announce his engagement at his mother's ball, if he was ever going to.

Noelle did not know what to expect. The Earl was like a gentle presence in the background, yet he still hadn't singled Ferne out. There had been other offers for Ferne, though, much to Winston's chagrin. The gentlemen asked *his* permission to seek her hand, and some of the men were older than Win, some were even his friends. He was mortified. After the first time, and after a council of Noelle, Taylor and Lady Wrenthe, it was decided that Win would refuse all offers that Taylor couldn't hint away at the door, until Ferne gave them the name of the man she would accept. This saved Ferne a great many awkward scenes and left the suitors some of their pride, but still put Win in a damnable position. He was tired of it and getting tired of the whole London scene, as he kept telling Nell. He was spending hours a day changing his clothes, when he should be checking on his crops. He was bored with slow canters down Rotten Row and itched for a cross-country gallop over his own lands. Besides, he declared angrily one morning at breakfast, he was fed up to here with the giggling, simpering debutantes batting their eyes at him behind their fans. The girls at home were never like this, putting on airs. He never felt comfortable with these die-away misses, not like good old Sally back at Squire's. Out of boredom and restlessness, Noelle supposed, he was drinking and gambling more, taking part in hair-raising escapades she only heard of when they were over. Win was no little boy she could admonish; she could only worry, telling him to be patient. They would be going home in a few weeks.

Noelle mentioned this to Ferne one rainy day when, for once, they were alone for tea. It didn't seem to matter to Ferne that her Season was almost over without her having accepted anyone, even when Noelle made sure her sister understood they could not afford another. Ferne only answered that she was happy in Derbyshire, too. It was great fun being an incomparable, but she would not want to marry any man she did not love. Noelle could not argue with that, even if the nice Mallon boy was worth an abbey and idolized Ferne. Noelle supposed that Ferne was also waiting for the Earl to come up to scratch. What if he didn't? When she tried to broach the topic, Ferne just brushed it aside. They had somehow lost the habit of easy confidences in all the rushing about, so Nell really couldn't gauge her sister's feelings, she realised sadly, or how deeply her emotions were engaged. Ferne was chattering on about Clarice, to whose home she had again been invited as soon as the Countess arrived as the Armstrongs' patroness. Ferne still visited Clarice frequently, even taking some of her new friends to cheer the invalid. She had been so successful that now James Waverly called on the Kingsleys himself, since Clarice had been allowed the downstairs parlour or the garden lounge. Of course Clarice was not yet Out, but next year should see them fixed, Ferne announced proudly. And Clarice had invited Ferne to stay at the Kingsleys' for Clarice's come-out ball, so Noelle did not need to look so downcast, after all . . . and could they have lobster patties at their own party next week?

When Ferne left to speak to Cook about the menu, Noelle

wandered to the window. Maybe it was the rain that had her blue-devilled, or exhaustion from all the partying. It was almost over, their glorious Season, she thought as she watched the spatters on the glass, and then what? Win would be glad to get home, but if the Earl did not declare himself Ferne's heart could be broken. Maybe it had been wrong to come. Ferne would have bloomed anywhere she was planted, if her spirit wasn't crushed. Even Aunt Hattie weighed guiltily on Noelle's mind. Her aunt was having the time of her life, organising ladies into knitting sessions by day, winning their pin money by night. She would most likely be miserable back in Derbyshire with nothing to do but mend sheets. Noelle had wanted so much better for all of them, she could not help feeling depressed, without even considering her own bleak future.

She would never marry; she knew that. She had had two kind offers herself, yet both men seemed callow, unpolished, compared to the Earl of Wrenthe. She'd tried to avoid admitting her foolish, wrongheaded love, even to herself, but she had to now, it hurt so badly. Maybe she could bear it if he married Ferne; at least her sister would be happy. To see him—Noelle would rather return to Derbyshire. If he didn't marry Ferne, there was still no hope, but more options. She could return to London when Winnie was settled and Ferne had her farmer, though Noelle didn't think she'd like living on the fringes of Society, after being at the pinnacle, and there just wasn't enough income to support this style for long. Perhaps she could take in boarders rather than be a burden on Win at Sterlingwood. Or else she could sell the house and use the money to set up a little establishment in Bath for her and Aunt Hattie, where they could sew up baby things. Or use the money to dower Ferne, so if she did come to London for a visit, she could hold her head a little higher. Noelle might even ask Lady Wrenthe if there was a place for her, helping with the foundlings, unless it meant seeing the Earl. It all came back to him. It always did.

Enough, she told herself. It's raining and you cannot go out; that is no excuse for this fit of the megrims. Why, that's all in the future, and there are enough plaguey details to worry over today, like the party we are giving.

She left the window, from which the whole world looked damp and muddy, and sat at her desk, sharpening a penpoint to make a list.

Ferne and Cook were organising the menu; Win was seeing about a small orchestra so they could have dancing. Taylor would take care of the wine and hiring more servants. She would have to speak to Sam about more grooms. Now *there* was a problem. She wrote *Sam* on the page next to *staff*. The coachman had stopped haunting brothels, thank goodness, since his mistresses were so busy, but he had not given up the search for his childhood sweetheart. Instead, once the Armstrongs were inside whichever great house they were invited to, Sam would skulk around the servants' entrance, looking for his Peggoty. When he was tossed out, as he invariably was, he haunted the lines of coaches waiting outside, positive one of the drivers must know of her. Since many of the answers he received were of a ribald nature, and since Sam was always ready to defend his love's good name, Noelle had the most battered-looking coachman in the city. There was no way Noelle had the heart to dismiss Sam—she had known him forever—so she'd tried to send him home. Sam had begged to stay, sure his Peg was nearby, somewhere. Sitting on the box at night, his hat pulled low, he didn't look as bad. He could not be allowed to hand ladies out of their coaches, however, else they would faint dead away on Noelle's doorstep.

Noelle underlined *Sam*. And drew a circle around it.

Flowers. Lady Wrenthe had offered to help, but Noelle did not want to accept. With the Countess's own, much grander, ball just a short while after the Armstrongs' modest entertainment, the Surrey gardeners would be planning for that. And Lady Wrenthe had done so much for them already.

Their dresses were next on the list. Ferne had an exquisite ball gown she hadn't worn yet, watercolour blue to match her eyes. Perhaps she had better save that for the Countess's ball, too. Noelle recalled some patterned China silk in one of the attic trunks they had unearthed, and she decided to consult *Les Cousines* about having it made up.

Last was the guest list itself. Noelle started a new sheet, busily writing the names of all their favourite people. The house could not hold a major squeeze, so the invitations had to be limited. There were the patronesses who had kindly invited the Armstrongs to Almack's, hostesses whose hospitality had to be returned. Happily, they most likely would not attend such a youthful gathering, at such short notice. Noelle reached for the first list and wrote *Card Room—Aunt Hattie*, just in case.

Returning to the guest list, Noelle idly twiddled with a curl, wrapping it around her finger as she deliberated. A few more names, a smudge on her cheek, oh, mustn't forget dear old Admiral Hayes. Another pause to think of anyone she'd missed.

One name she would *not* include was Sir Rupert Dynhoff, yet another stormcloud on this wretched day. The man appeared everywhere, though no one seemed to like him. As part of the Prince's circle he had entrée to all the major functions. Noelle had been warned he was a rake, but what could she do? The man persisted in paying attention to Ferne. Not enough to be offensive, yet Noelle noticed how his dampish eyes kept watching Ferne, no matter what else he was doing, and it made her uneasy. Ferne didn't care for him either, he reminded her of oysters, but she didn't know how to discourage him. If Ferne refused him a dance, he would stare at her all night, so it was easier to accept. He never went beyond the bounds, so Ferne didn't really mind. Noelle did. Dynhoff was known to be a gambler, a wastrel. He could only be hanging out for an heiress, which everyone knew Ferne wasn't. His intentions could not be honourable, so his presence was an affront.

Noelle was rude to him, hoping he would take the point, and had Taylor deny him the house. A man with his reputation must be privately received very rarely, so he could not have been surprised, yet he seemed to sneer at Noelle, then edge a little closer to Ferne. Nell was afraid to discuss Dynhoff with Winnie, for fear he would then challenge the older man. It was just as well Win spent more time in the card rooms than he did at his sister's side. Pistols for two and breakfast for one was *not* a proper solution, in Noelle's estimation, especially if that one was bound to be the experienced libertine. Noelle wished she could ask Wrenthe, who was awake on all suits. He could certainly handle himself in any situation; even a loose fish like Dynhoff would respect the Earl.

Noelle could not ask Wrenthe, however. They were not on

such familiar terms, for one thing. Her pride would not let her go to him with yet another of her problems, for a second. He had once said she was incompetent to run her family, making micefeet of their affairs. Well, they hadn't been in any scrapes since, which ought to prove something. Besides, if he was interested in Ferne himself, he would make sure Dynhoff kept his distance. The Season had only a few short weeks to go; they could tolerate the man for that long.

Noelle had underestimated Sir Rupert, just as she had overestimated Wrenthe. Ferne had become an obsession with the dissolute Dynhoff. He was bound and determined to have her, one way or the other. At every rebuff of Noelle's, every time her nose-in-the-air butler slammed the door in his face, he veered closer to the other.

The Earl, meanwhile, had not even noticed Dynhoff. He was too busy watching Noelle to notice who danced with Ferne, much less who ogled the little ninnyhammer. Dynhoff was a cad and a bounder, but no one could blame him if he had an eye for beauty. No, the Earl was too concerned with Noelle and Millbrooke, Noelle and the Lieutenant, Noelle and—

He knew for a fact Noelle had already refused Harcourt, Taylor not being above bribery. Somehow he felt she would not accept anyone until Ferne was settled, and with the Season closing maybe the widgeon would accept one of her beaus. The Earl was waiting. It was safer that way, since it hadn't gone away, this disastrous intrusion into his neat, ordered life. He'd thought it might, if he avoided the source of his discomfort. Then he could return to his own peaceful, easygoing pursuits, without any more of those tumultuous episodes. But he'd been wrong. A head cold you could get over in a week; infatuation took a little longer; and love, well, it looked like love was going to be forever, and the Earl was nervous. If truth be told, he was positively quaking; that's why he was waiting.

They were always brangling . . . maybe he couldn't live with her. Lord, could he live without her? And what if she turned him down?

Simple, he'd let his beard grow, build a grotto somewhere and become a hermit.

=== 13 ===
DEAR OLD TAYLOR

"OH MUM, YOU look a treat, y'do."

"It's not too, er, different, Janie?"

"Well, I never saw the like, mum, if that's what you mean, not in all those magazines Miss Ferne showed me. But it's prettier nor any, I vow. You look like a regular princess, if there be princesses in that heathen place."

Noelle could not agree with the last. Whoever heard of a Chinese princess with red-brown hair and green eyes? Besides, she was sure that the French modistes' interpretation of the kimono style would hardly be recognizable to a real Oriental. *Les Cousines*, two of them at any rate, had broken into an excited, rapid, dialect French, undecipherable to Noelle, after their first rapture at seeing her bolt of fabric. A heavy black silk, it was, with large white birds in flight around flame-coloured vines, and all picked out in gold stitches.

What they had created, Noelle feared, was something like a man's dressing gown, a large man at that. The sleeves were so wide and so long she was afraid for the turtle soup at dinner. The front panels met and crossed indecently low on her chest, revealing a startling expanse of pale skin before tying in some fiendish little gold bows down one side that somehow managed to pull the fabric taut across her breasts and hips. On her ears she wore long gold earrings shaped like leaves, and in her hair a black feathered headband she and Ferne had spent hours gluing together. Gold sandals completed the outfit, except for a last quick dusting of powder across her cheeks. Oriental princess or waif dressed—or undressed—in a man's bathrobe, she would have to do. Her guests would be arriving at any minute. After a few final words to Janie, who would have to be on duty with

Moira in case any of the lady guests needed assistance, Noelle went downstairs.

On her way to the Chinese room where, on a dramatic impulse, she had elected to receive her guests, she adjusted the large bowl of roses on the hall table. The Countess had insisted the blooms would not last another ten days, so there was no reason for Noelle to toss away good money when they'd only land in the gardener's compost. Red, white and the palest pink, Noelle had arranged them in a large Crown Derby Porcelain vase with two handles that she had toted all the way to London, along with a Derby harlequin, as reminders of home.

She meant to have a word with Taylor, not that there was anything left undone at this point, but he was not in sight. One of the young footmen was near the doorway in his place, using his sleeve to put a finishing sheen on the brass buttons of his livery. The footman appeared to be just as nervous as his mistress, at this first major entertainment. Too tense to just sit, Noelle took a last tour of the drawing rooms. The smaller parlour, where they often received visitors, was already set up with deal tables at one end and the sofas at the other to provide a quiet conversation area. The Armstrongs had seldom used the other, formal salon; it was too cold, too bare. They had removed Aunt Sylvia's artifacts, but used the better attic finds in the smaller, cosier rooms. They had decided against refurbishing this large room, weighing the use they would have for it versus all the other expenses. As a result this vast expanse always seemed unfinished, unfriendly. It echoed, Noelle felt, with Aunt Sylvia's ill will. Now it was transformed. The chandelier had been taken down and polished until its prisms made rainbows out of the candlelight. A huge fire burned at one end to take the chill off; the small orchestra would sit at the other. Gilt ballroom chairs, borrowed from Lady Brock for the occasion, stood against the walls, which were decorated with swags of greenery caught in pink streamers, with here and there a gilded basket full of trailing roses. Aunt Sylvia's ghost would have to learn to waltz, Noelle decided with a giggle, unless the shade took up residence with the stuffed crocodiles in the attic.

The room adjoining the newly named ballroom was to be

used for the late-night supper, Ferne's lobster patties included. The Waterford goblets sparkled, the crested silver and the Sèvres china were lined up on the white linen in readiness. More flowers, more candles . . . why, one footman was assigned to do nothing but trim wicks in all the rooms. Another's duty was to circle the rooms with trays of champagne glasses. There were three kitchen helpers hired for the evening who would also help serve; two tall footmen stationed in the hallway—for what reason Noelle didn't know—Taylor said they lent dignity; three parlourmaids in new black uniforms with frilly, starched caps and aprons, to keep things tidy; the two ladies' maids up-stairs to help refresh the females. There were people to take the guests' wraps, people to hold carriage doors, people to direct other people, and all under Taylor's command. As for cost, there were more candles burning than they'd use in Derbyshire for a year, and Noelle wouldn't be surprised if she had more persons in her employ this one evening than she had coming as guests.

Right now everything was very still, almost hushed in ex-pectancy, even the rustling of her gown. The servants must be at their own meal, she realised, enjoying the last few moments before the dinner guests started to arrive. She gave one more fond look around. It was all perfect, and it was all hers. Whatever the expense, it was worth it.

Her family was already gathered in the Chinese room, and as Noelle stood in the doorway she felt pride swell up inside her like a balloon. This, too, was worth anything. Whatever happened later, she would always have this memory: Ferne like a wood nymph in palest green lustring, poised and confident, no longer blushing and tongue-tied in company; Win in elegant evening dress with lace at his wrists, instead of in stained buckskins and corduroys, actually conversing about something other than hogs, sheep or chickens; and Aunt Hattie, no longer a dumpy, dizzy, addlepate, but a dignified, sophisticated matron in her grey satin, sipping a sherry. It wasn't the clothes, merely, or the new self-assurance that meant so much to Noelle. They were *happy*, that's what mattered. They were looking forward to an evening of good friends and good conversation, a cut-throat game of penny-ante cards, an innocent game of mild flirtation perhaps, things they had not had in Derbyshire.

There was only one disturbing accent in this picture, a small, white one.

"Ferne, what is that dog doing here? You know we can't have them down tonight! I made sure Plato was in my room."

"But, Nellie, I spent all afternoon bathing and combing them! Couldn't Jasmine just stay to greet the guests? After all, she is part of the family."

Winnie laughed. Exasperation mixed with amusement for Noelle, too. "Dearest, even children are excused from evening parties in most 'families.' And you know how Jasmine is always begging for food or trying to climb into someone's lap."

"But, Nell—"

"No. No. No. What if she got stepped on?"

That did it. Ferne hurried to shut the dog in with Noelle's, returning to the Chinese room just as the door knocker was sounding.

There would be over fifty guests later in the evening, but only twenty were invited to dinner. They were all having sherry or Madeira, ratafia for the younger ladies, chatting companionably while the Armstrongs made certain everyone was introduced around. When Taylor entered the room, looking more aristocratic than the Earl, even, in his black butler suit and powdered wig, Noelle thought it was to announce dinner. It was a trifle early, but all of the guests were present. Taylor caught her eye, however, and gestured minutely towards the hall.

Excusing herself to Admiral Hayes, Noelle followed Taylor to the deserted corridor.

"What is it, Taylor? You don't look quite well." Indeed the butler seemed a bit pale. "Is something wrong?"

"I am afraid we have a slight problem, Miss Noelle."

"A problem? Has Cook burned the mutton?"

Taylor harrumphed indignantly. "I am afraid it is a little more serious than that, madam."

"Well what is it, Taylor? We have twenty people in there waiting for their dinner. If the house is on fire, tell me now!"

"It is not as drastic as that." He cleared his throat as Noelle was getting ready to shout or stamp her foot or—"I have received word that someone has informed the excise office of contraband in this vicinity. There is to be a house-to-house search this evening."

Militiamen in her ballroom? Looking under the table during dinner? It would be better if the house *were* on fire. Trying very hard not to go off in an apoplectic fit, Noelle slowly, quietly, ever so politely, asked, "And will the officers find anything in my house, Taylor?"

Taylor looked down his nose at her. "Certainly not, madam."

"Not in the cellars? The attics?"

"Most assuredly not."

"The stables, Taylor? Dear Lord, please not the stables!"

Taylor shook his head. Noelle's heart started pumping blood again. In relief she even smiled at him. Dear old Taylor.

"Well, then," she said, "it may be a bit awkward, but I shall just explain to the guests that the soldiers must have their foolish hunt, and that will be that. We have no problem."

"No, madam." No smile either. "But Lady Bromley might."

"Lady Bromley, who owns the house next door—the one that's been empty since we got here, with the knocker off the door?"

"Yes, miss. The lady was visiting in Scotland, I believe. I happened to have a talk with the caretaker this noon. It seems Lady Bromley is arrived in Town today. She'll put up at Grillon's Hotel tonight."

"Why are you telling me this, Taylor? I have a countess, an earl and an admiral in there, besides countless other titles," she almost shouted. "I don't *care* which hotel Lady Bromley is staying at!"

"No, ma'am." Taylor took a very audible breath. "She will send her staff over at first light to air the rooms, make up the beds, remove the Holland covers from the furniture . . ."

". . . And?"

Taylor gave one conscious look at Noelle before fixing his

sight a foot or so above her head. "And there are certain, ah, unexpected items under the Holland covers."

Noelle gasped. "You mean you have been hiding smuggled goods in the lady's drawing room?"

A nod. "Under ordinary circumstances the, ah, merchandise was to have been removed this evening during dinner—"

"The extra footmen?" Noelle's body seemed paralysed; she was not yet brain-numb.

"Exactly," Taylor admitted with a glimmer of respect. "But now . . ."

"Now you cannot move it, not with riding officers in the neighbourhood. So either they will find it and trace it here, or Lady Bromley's people will discover it and raise the dust?"

Taylor stood mute, staring at the wall. Noelle wondered if they would deport her. Dear Lord, wasn't smuggling a hanging offence? Would they believe she didn't know anything about her butler's free trading? Even *she* didn't believe that: the silk, the wine. No, it would be Australia for her. They would drag her from the ballroom and the Earl would raise his quizzing glass to stare at her, telling his dancing partner, "I always thought there was something dashed irregular about those Armstrongs."

Those Armstrongs! Good grief, would they arrest Ferne and Win, too? A hysterical giggle escaped her as she imagined Aunt Hattie knitting sweaters for kangaroos or whatever they called those peculiar creatures in Australia.

Taylor seemed to disapprove of the giggle. "Miss Noelle, may I suggest—"

"Taylor," she said, standing very straight, "I do not believe I wish to hear any more suggestions from you. See any more of you. Have anything whatsoever more to do with you. At all, ever. Is that clear?"

"Quite, madam. However, your father—"

"My father, Taylor, was a charming, irresponsible fool who was only saved from ruin by his work in the Foreign Office. All that he bequeathed to us was you, to complete the job. If he were here now, he would most likely be hand in glove with you in this. If he were here, though, and if he were any kind of natural father, he would take you out and shoot you. Which is exactly what I intend to do tomorrow, if you are still here and I am not aboard a ship for Botany Bay.

"Right now," she announced, her head held high and proud as she turned her back on him, "I am going to rejoin my guests for a delightful repast, scintillating conversation and sparkling wit. If I do not faint."

Noelle did not drag her sleeve in the turtle soup, spill her wine or drop her fork each time she heard a noise in the hallway. She did not commit any social gaffes over dinner that might offend the Earl of Wrenthe, seated on her right, or Admiral Hayes, on her left, as the two highest ranking gentlemen. She even managed to sound fairly informed about the war, between the mutton and the roast pheasant; about Miss Austen's latest book, during sliced ham with asparagus. Of course she did not taste any of the food or hear any of the conversation, as she waited for her door to burst inwards, soldiers advancing, bayonets at the ready. For once the Earl was not the centre of her focus. She was aware of him looking superb, as always, perhaps a little more grey at the temples than she remembered. No, that must be her imagination, running amok under fire. She was also aware of his quizzing expression, those dark brows raised in curiosity. He was too well mannered to say anything about her fidgets, and for once Noelle didn't care what he thought. It was quite obvious what the Earl would think if the revenuers arrested his hosts.

Noelle felt as if she'd been severed in two. One part of her was making sure that course followed smoothly after course, the perfect hostess seeing to her guests' needs. The second part of her was somewhere over the tapestried wall, looking down and pulling the hostess's strings. This second Noelle, divorced from the Chinese princess, was also making plans to flee, to plead, to lie through her teeth if need be. This other self plotted and raged and wept.

Noelle smiled at the Admiral. "Wait until you see the dessert. I hope you'll like it."

Taylor wheeled in a cart with a silver dish of strawberry trifle in brandy. During the hush in conversation he ceremoniously lighted the dish with a long taper. As it went up in blue flames all of the guests oohed and aahed. One Noelle accepted the praise with gratitude. The other Noelle, the one whose insides were mush, only thought: And the bastard's hand didn't even shake. Dear old Taylor.

The ladies retired to the Chinese room, leaving the men to their port and cigars. Ferne and two friends took turns at the pianoforte, singing soft country airs while the older women gossipped. Lady Wrenthe thought Noelle looked peaked, but Nell was able to convince her it was just from all the preparations for the party.

"Well, don't wear yourself to a frazzle, girl," the Countess told her, "that's what you've got servants for."

If she fainted, Noelle wondered, would they all go home? She wasn't that pudding-hearted. Besides, she'd got her knees locked so tight to keep them from shaking, she doubted she could walk, much less fall. It was too late anyway, the men were returning. The Earl came straight to her side, looking concerned. Drat the man, she thought. Why did he have to pick tonight of all nights to look at her so tenderly? Let him go smile at Ferne and see if *her* heart melted. Noelle for one needed all her wits about her. She excused herself. She thought the Countess was signalling for her. The Earl's brows knit together.

An eternity later it was time for Noelle to lead the way to the ballroom, to stand just inside it with her aunt and her brother, to receive the rest of the guests, leaving Ferne to circulate among the company and make introductions. Noelle wanted to clutch Winnie's arm, but he needed it to shake hands with. She flinched each time she heard the front door opening. . . . There would be a pause while the wraps were taken, then Taylor's voice would intone: "Lord and Lady Hanson," or "Sir Francis Goshorn," or "His grace, the Duke of Carlyle" etc. Noelle curtsied, she smiled, she had her hand kissed . . . forever. The next name, no, the one after, was going to be it: Sergeant Smith, His Majesty's Army, arresting officer. But it wasn't, and then all the expected—make that invited—guests had arrived and it was time to start the dancing. Somehow she got through that too, all eyes on her as she led off with Wrenthe, again a courtesy to his title. She accepted his compliments on her gown, the dinner, the ballroom, her banana trees.

"My banana trees, sir?"

"I just wanted to see if you were paying attention. You seem a little, um, abstracted."

"Oh la, sir, what a tease," she twitted, angry at herself for imitating those lisping flirts she despised, but the ploy seemed to work. The Earl made innocuous small talk for the rest of the set. She had only to murmur occasional agreement to his remarks about the Parthenon marbles at the British Museum. How beautiful they were, and how perfect, and how ancient. Of course she'd never got around to seeing them, which was obvious to Wrenthe, but it got her through the dance.

After that she declined to take the floor until later. She excused herself with the pretense of having to see to her company first. That way she was free to move from group to group, smiling and adding bits to the conversations without having to concentrate. The whist players were too engrossed to notice her. Lieutenant Ramsey and two junior cavalry officers seemed to be enacting Wellington's strategies with the silverware in the supper room; knives for the English, forks for the French, spoons for the Prussians. Noelle passed by without interrupting.

She decided, on her way back to the ballroom, that it was all a hum. She did not know where Taylor had got his information from, but she could be sure it was no legitimate source. The Excise Bureau could not make a practise of announcing their plans for inspections beforehand. No, the informant was suspect, so must be the information. Putting Lady Bromley from her mind, she accepted a dance with Lord Brock. Three dances later, when she was just beginning to enjoy herself, she felt the tap of doom on her shoulder—Taylor requesting her presence outside, if you please, ma'am.

Thankfully, no guests wandered the corridors at that moment, for there were the Sergeant and three of his men. The officer was young—she hadn't expected that—and embarrassed. His name was Eagan, Sergeant Walter Eagan of the Home Guard.

"I am very sorry, ma'am, but an information has been laid concerning smuggled goods, so I have been ordered to search the premises. I truly regret it, ma'am.'' He did regret it, whole-heartedly. He was a soldier, with nothing to do with any of the nobility, and here he was, barging into some lady's party. Such a pretty lady too, though the nobs had strange ideas of propriety if they let their women wear outfits like that. That black thing was cut so low you could almost see—

"Sergeant!" He raised his eyes in time to see her nose lift haughtily in the air. "I have over fifty guests here this evening. They are drinking champagne, sherry and claret. Do you wish to see the bills from the wine merchant?''

The Sergeant gulped. "No, ma'am. I'm just supposed to in-stitute a search, nothing else.''

"I have some very important guests. Do you intend to search them, too?''

"Lord, no, Miss Armstrong. That's no part of my orders.'' He blanched at the thought. Half those carriages outside had crests. "I wouldn't need to go anywheres near the company rooms, ma'am, just the attics and pantries like.''

Noelle decided to be condescending, since she had few other options: "Very well. It is thoroughly tiresome and in-convenient, and I shall have a word with your superiors tomorrow, but I realize they have to do something about all this abominable smuggling. Don't those criminals know the blockade of France is for the country's good?''

" 'xactly, ma'am, and I thank you for being so un-derstanding.''

"Not at all, you must do your job. I merely ask that you be about it as quickly as possible, so my guests are not alarmed.''

"Oh no, ma'am, I wouldn't want that. Jenkins, you take the stables out back; Skell, you get the attics; Brown, the cellars. That is, ma'am, if you'd be so kind as to have someone direct my men?''

"Certainly. I would not want them frightening my maids on the back stairs. Taylor, see to it. Make sure the men fetch candles also.'' Taylor nodded, motioning for the soldiers to follow him to the rear of the house. Noelle had no idea what she was to do with Sergeant Eagan now; she offered him a glass of wine.

"No, thank you, ma'am, very kind and all, considering the

circumstances. But not on duty." He shifted his weight from one foot to the other. "Do you think I might inspect the pantries, though? That way my report will be all right and tight, the way the Captain likes."

"Of course. I'll escort you myself. Perhaps I may even be able to persuade you to try the claret cup." Seeing Taylor returning to resume his position in the hall, Noelle smiled up at the young officer before adding, with a touch of honey, "Unless you feel that small refreshment might interfere with your next search?"

The Sergeant blushed. "No, ma'am, this is the last for the night. We're to report back to the Captain."

"How nice," Noelle said, winking at Taylor as she passed him in the hall.

The Sergeant followed her towards the kitchens, staring wide-eyed as he caught glimpses of the reception rooms through open doors. It was true then; some of those ladies were half naked in those gauzy things.

Hurrying him along, Noelle casually inquired into the informant, "For of course there are no illegal goods here, so it must have been a mistaken address, an error on someone's part." The Sergeant was happy to agree with this beautiful woman with the big . . . eyes . . . about her probable innocence, yet he wasn't helpful about the other matter.

"No, ma'am, he gave us the address, and the name, real specific like."

"But your superiors must have considered that it might be a malicious prank," she persisted, "a spiteful servant who'd been turned off, or a merchant left unpaid or some such thing?"

"No way, ma'am. The informant were a gentleman, that I know."

"A gentleman? Like a lord, you mean?"

"I don't know about a title; I didn't hear no names. But he was dressed to the nines, he was, and had the Captain yes-sirrin' and no-sirrin' him all over the place."

Noelle did manage to convince Sergeant Eagan there would be no harm in just a small glass of champagne, after his brief check of the pantries, while they waited for his men. Especially, she said, ". . . Since you are so close to being off duty."

Hearing this, Cook even wrapped up a few strawberry tarts left over from tea for the officer and his men, declaring how she admired a "young man what has a care for his dooty."

The Earl of Wrenthe was not enjoying the party. He was not dancing, gaming or eating. He was lounging by the ballroom door, brooding. Something was wrong here, and he was going to find out what. In the past, he would have ignored such goings-on as none of his concern, or sent a lackey to see to it. Now, he realized, everything relating to Miss Armstrong concerned him, especially anything that caused her to worry or kept her from his side. When Noelle did not return to the dancing, he stepped outside to the hall, in time to see her walk down the corridor with a revenue officer. Taylor was mopping his forehead. The Earl quirked one imperious eyebrow at him.

There was no point in dissembling, Taylor knew. Lord Wrenthe had only to stop by Lord Liverpool's office in the morning to find all the information he wanted. That he *did* want the information was obvious from the uncomfortable silence. Looking straight ahead, Taylor complied:

"It seems, my lord, that the Excise Bureau received a warning this afternoon concerning contraband in the vicinity. A dastardly lie, Lord Wrenthe."

The eyebrows rose a fraction. "Indeed?"

"Indeed. Miss Noelle has just escorted the Sergeant to the kitchens, where he will rejoin his men before informing his superiors of that fact. A minor inconvenience, my lord, that is all."

The Earl thought back to dinner, even before, when Noelle was edgy and wan-looking. Her behaviour all night reminded him of an injured bird, fluttering around in circles, trying to get airborne. Excise men coming to the house could do that to a person, if she knew beforehand, and if she had anything to hide.

"Taylor," he asked, "is Miss Noelle involved in your, ah, business transactions?"

Taylor looked aghast. "Certainly not, my lord. Tonight was merely unfortunate in that I felt she must be informed, what with the company and all."

"And the men won't find anything here?"

"No, my lord."

After more reflection Wrenthe concluded that Noelle would be unscathed, if shaken, and not well pleased to see him snooping in her corridors. Before returning to the ballroom, however, he had one more question for the butler:

"You do know, don't you, Taylor, that smuggling, or handling smuggled goods, is against the law?"

"My lord," Taylor answered in a pained voice, "for the last six years I have lived with my sister and her children in Sussex. Her husband was a soldier who died for his country, and the Crown gives them nothing. We lived on my pension and what washing my sister could take in. Free trading's illegal, you say? It is a way of life along that coast. That's all the rocks and inlets are good for. There they say that you don't get hung for running the blockade; you get hung for getting caught. It may be wrong, but not as wrong as letting good people go hungry, that I know."

"But you have involved the Armstrongs this time."

"And I sorely regret that." Brightening, Taylor added, "That Miss Noelle, though. She is pluck to the backbone. You should have seen—"

"It is going to stop." There was no question, merely a bare statement of fact. Wrenthe held up his hand before Taylor could say anything. "I do not wish to know anything whatsoever about your dealings—I have compromised myself as it is—but this must not continue. You were lucky tonight, I assume. It might not go so well the next time."

"There will not be a next time, my lord. You have my word on it. This was the last shipment either way. I have been saving and now have enough to set myself up in business."

"Oh?" Wrenthe spoke with some disquietude.

"I always wanted to run a gaming house. A very select establishment, naturally. My sister would be provided for, there would be jobs for the youngsters and, if I may say so, opportunities for me to utilize my particular skills."

"An excellent notion, Taylor! You'll give White's and Watier's a run for their money. Let me know and I'll be your first patron . . . but what of the Armstrongs?"

"Oh, I wouldn't dream of leaving the Ambassador's family, my lord, until the ladies are . . . ahem . . . settled."

Wrenthe coloured slightly and cleared *his* throat. Taylor pointedly led the way back to the ballroom, saying only, "Quite so, my lord."

=== 14 ===
DAWNING

THE GUESTS WERE gone at last. The good-byes had seemed to go on forever, everyone telling Noelle what a bang-up affair the evening had been. It must have been; they stayed past three. With dawn a few short hours away, she hurried her family off to bed, and dismissed all of the staff to their quarters, announcing that morning was soon enough to begin the cleanup. When everyone was out of range she asked Taylor about the militiamen.

"Oh, they left soon enough, Miss Noelle, that young Sergeant singing your praises. I had one of the lads follow them—straight back to the barracks."

"What a relief! What about Lady Bromley?"

"Lady Bromley's house shall be, ah, presentable by daybreak. As soon as the family is abed . . ."

"Yes, well, I'll go hurry them along. Ferne would stay up for hours, otherwise, dancing every set again."

As she started up the stairs, Taylor bid her good night: "And I just wish to add, Miss Noelle, that you were a regular trooper. The Ambassador would have been proud."

Her earlier words forgotten, Noelle turned and beamed at him. "Yes, I believe he would!"

Once upstairs, Noelle pleaded a headache to get Ferne, already in her nightclothes, back into her own bedroom. She added the admonition that Ferne should not keep poor Aunt Hattie awake either, with her chatter, nor Moira, who had to be up early in the morning. Noelle sent a yawning Janie to sleep, saying she was quite capable of undoing the few bows that held her gown together and untying her slippers. She was only in her petticoat when Janie turned the bed down and left. Noelle counted to one hundred, very slowly, before jumping up and yanking open the wardrobe. She pulled out an old brown merino from the country and tossed it over her head, grabbed up an old shawl and knotted it in front. A worn pair of shoes in her hand and she was ready. She put her ear to the door, counted another one hundred, backwards, then tiptoed down the stairs.

They were all in the kitchen, Taylor, Cook, Moira, stable-hands and grooms, sitting quietly around the table. Everyone jumped up when they saw Noelle, but she shushed their exclamations.

"It's all right. I've come to help."

"But Miss Noelle," Taylor remonstrated indignantly, "it would not be proper!"

"*Now* you worry about what's proper? Taylor, sometimes you amaze me. I—"

Noelle did not finish because just then came the sound of a carriage leaving the stables. The servants all filed out silently, Moira turning to curtsey to Noelle, her eyes twinkling. Noelle slapped the shoes on her feet and hurried after them.

Three vehicles were lined up in the rear roadway where deliveries were usually made: The Armstrongs' heavy old travelling coach with Sam at the reins, his hat pulled low, the kitchen wagon and another closed carriage, evidently hired. How Taylor happened to have the key to Lady Bromley's rear entrance Noelle did not want to know, but soon they were inside, with only a few covered lanterns to light the way.

"This is the dicey part, miss," Moira told her, as if Noelle didn't realise it. "We don't want the watch seeing any lights from an empty house. Of course one of the lads be on lookout up at the corner . . ."

Taylor was directing the men to various areas of the house. Noelle followed Moira's light to the drawing room, where they peeked under each Holland cover, being careful not to disturb the ones on end tables, sofas, tea carts and tambour frames. Soon there was a silent pass-along line formed, all those extra footmen and grooms handing keg and crate down the hall, out the kitchen, into the wagon. When the wagon was filled it moved off and the hired carriage took its place. Noelle and Moira stayed a few steps ahead of the men, pointing out the contraband. When the second coach held its limit, Taylor told the two women to go off home. They were almost finished anyway, and both had to make an appearance tomorrow for the family. Noelle could hardly keep her eyes open, much less argue, so she was glad to follow Moira back to their own kitchen, then up to bed.

There was a murky greyness in the air—London dawn—when Taylor made one final check of the premises before sending off the rest of the staff and waving Sam forward with the last load.

As Taylor turned the key in the back door lock, two carriages drove up to the front entrance, delivering Lady Bromley's housekeeper, the French chef, three footmen and two maids, and a quantity of baggage. The younger maid, a plump girl with bright-red braids and a chipped front tooth, stood in the street admiring her fine new London residence until the housekeeper gave her a nudge. She hurried to fetch in the covered bird cage, wondering where the neighbours could be off to, so early in the morning.

It was one day before the house was back in order, two days before Noelle felt alive again, and three days before Sam was back "from having the old carriage repaired."

That afternoon, while Aunt Hattie was out paying calls and Ferne was visiting Clarice, Jasmine and Janie along with her, and Win was somewhere watching a mill—foul sport—Noelle thought she would try to settle her accounts. She was just gathering all the tradesmen's bills together in a neat stack when Cook's scullery maid staggered into the room.

"Mum, mum," she cried, wringing her apron in her hands, "it's Sam. In the kitchen, with blood all over and him a-weepin' and a-cryin' about goin' off t'die. And Cook, she fainted dead away and the beans is all over the floor and I don' know what to do!" She threw the apron over her head and blubbered into it.

Noelle jerked the apron down and shouted at the girl: "What you will *not* do is get hysterical. Go find Taylor and send him to me in the kitchen. Then get one of the maids to

141

fetch towels and hot water. And smelling salts. Now move it, girl!''

Things were not quite as dire in the kitchen as Noelle had pictured. Sam was sitting at the table, a sorry sight indeed, tears mingling with great splashes of blood, but obviously not at death's door. Cook was standing amid the beans, pale and shaky, but standing. Taylor arrived, took instant stock of the situation, and reached a bottle down from the shelf. Pouring two glasses, he set one in front of Sam, who only moaned. He put the other glass in Cook's hand and, his arm around her cushiony shoulder, led her from the room, murmuring about his little pigeon. Little pigeon? Cook was at least twice Noelle's weight! She'd have to see about that, later.

A maid came in with towels and a pitcher, but she screamed when she saw the bloody mess that was Sam, so Noelle told her to leave the things and get out. The scullion was sniffling over the beans and a dust pan.

''Sam, can you hear me, Sam?'' Noelle took up a towel and dipped it in the water, but she didn't know where to start. ''At least lift your head so I can—Oh heavens, I think your nose must be broken, Sam. Let me go send for the doctor, I'll be right back.''

''No, Miss Nell, just give me my quarter's pay and I'll go. I'm no use to you here, no use to anyone. I'll just go on home to Derbyshire.''

''You'll do no such thing, Sam. You're in no condition to travel. Here, put your head back so the bleeding will stop. You, child—Daisy, is it?—go tell one of the grooms to send for the doctor.''

Poor little Daisy, facing her mistress face-to-face for almost the first time, dropped what she was doing to obey the new orders. Which meant the beans were all over the floor again.

Thoroughly bemused by what went on in her own kitchen, Noelle stared after her.

''Don't fault the girl, Miss Nell. It's me. They can't stand to look at me,'' Sam wailed.

Taking a deep breath, Noelle sat at the table. ''Sam, do you think you are able to tell me what happened? Was it footpads? Did it have anything to do with, you know, the other night?''

''Nay, 'tweren't none of that, Miss Nell. It was Peg. My own

Peggoty Gallagher. She . . . she broke my nose and my heart both!'' He started to sob.

Noelle took one more look at Sam, one look at the glass Taylor had poured, and downed the whole thing. She'd have to ask Taylor about that, too. She was no connoisseur, but the kitchen sherry seemed better than the family's! She started to dab ineffectually at Sam's head, afraid of hurting him worse. She positioned one of his hands to hold a damp towel to his nose, at least stopping that blood bath for a time. She managed to locate a deep cut over his left eye and put his other hand there with a towel, too. There were smaller cuts and bruises, and he would have at least one black eye, again. His jaw was starting to discolour and the inside lip was dribbling blood. There was also a great lump at the back of Sam's head.

Eventually Noelle had him halfway cleaned up, using the pitcher and the pot Cook was intending for the beans. Then Sam started to tell his story. Between the towel at his nose, the swelling lip and his moaning, the tale was nearly incoherent at first. As best she could make out, Sam had driven Aunt Hattie to Mrs. Colter's and Ferne and company to the Kingsleys', then come home. Since he was not supposed to fetch the ladies until late in the afternoon, and no one else seemed to be needing his services, he had decided to introduce himself to the chap next door, Lady Bromley's head coachman. Friendly like, Sam had taken a pint over with him, which was followed by a second of the fellow Jed's providing. What with one thing and another, Sam came to tell Jed of his problems in trying to locate his dear lost Peggoty Gallagher. He'd no sooner mentioned the chipped tooth than Jed jumped up and slapped him on the back. She was there, right inside, this very minute!

Sam rushed right through Lady Bromley's back door, having had previous acquaintance with it, and found his Peggoty, after all that time . . . smack in the middle of the kitchen, in the arms of the French chef!

''Don't worry, Peg, I'll save you!'' he shouted, squaring off and landing the chef a mighty blow to the shoulder. The chef staggered but recovered. He hauled off and smashed one to Sam's jaw. Sam retaliated with a succession of blows, then a oner to the breadbasket, which sent the chef down and out.

During all of this, Peggoty had been screaming ''Pierre!

Pierre!'' Now she took a stance over her fallen hero, metal skillet in her hand, and started shouting at Sam, how she was engaged to Pierre and what had Sam done to him? Sam tried to explain, how he loved her, how *they* were going to get married. He had looked everywhere for her, he pleaded, all the employment bureaus, all the fancy mansions, all the brothels. That's when Peggoty started beating on his head with the cast-iron skillet. Got his nose with the first crack, she did, shrieking the whole time. Sam finally got the pan away from her when tap . . . tap . . . tap . . . this old lady came in on her cane. The chef was groaning on the floor; Peggoty was exercising her lungs. The old woman, Lady Bromley, took one look at the situation and lit into poor Sam with the cane. At that point pal Jed came in from the stables, hearing all the ruckus, to discover his mistress under attack by a madman. Finding the pint bottle still in his hand, he brought it down on the back of Sam's head. Two grooms had dragged the semiconscious Sam home . . .

". . . to die, Miss Nell, that's all I want to do.''

"Stop that nonsense this instant, Sam. I won't hear another word. You sit right here and wait for the doctor and I—I'll send Moira to sit with you. You know, Sam, we've all been so worried about you, but none more than Moira. She once told me she didn't understand how any woman could go off and leave you. She's a good, sensible girl, our Moira.'' Seeing that Sam was looking thoughtful, at least, Noelle added, "She's a decent, loyal girl. I'm sure she'd make some good man a fine, loving wife. You think about it, Sam, while I go get her.''

The door stood open at the Armstrong residence; no groom came to take the Earl's horses. Handing the reins to his tiger, telling him to walk the team, Wrenthe bounded up the stairs, through the entryway. No Taylor, no footmen. Good grief, had they all been taken to gaol? He walked down the empty corridor, his Hessian boots making echoes in the stillness. Then he saw her: huddled against the wall, her shoulders shaking, blood all over her gown. Dear God, he was too late!

"Nellie, darling, are you all right?'' he cried, throwing his arms around her. "What happened? Where is everyone? Do you need a doctor? The watch?''

Noelle almost missed the first part of this impassioned speech, she'd been laughing so hard. Pushing him away so she could wipe the tears from her eyes, she tried to get control of herself, but the Earl's expression was too much for her. What he must have thought! She went off again in spasms of dimpled hilarity.

"I'm so sorry, Lord Wrenthe," she gasped out finally. "I am truly not demented. Sam, our coachman, has had his nose broken and Taylor is, um, comforting Cook, so the house is at sixes and sevens. Will you please forgive us? I'll just go change—I realize I must have given you quite a fright—and send Moira down to poor Sam. Would you mind waiting in the parlour? Unless you came to see Ferne, of course. She's out for the afternoon."

Assured that, no, the Earl did not mind waiting, as long as there was no mayhem around him, and no, he hadn't called just to see Miss Ferne, Noelle tripped up the stairs, promising a full explanation when she was presentable again.

This had to be the most hobbledehoy household he'd ever seen, Wrenthe decided. He'd spent all morning, with no results, trying to find the identity of the revenuers' informant—and now this. He must have taken three steps closer to the grave, seeing Noelle in such a state! He knew he'd been ready to kill any man who would harm her; the bloodlust was only now ebbing away, leaving him shaken but sure. Sure he would have to make her his, and soon, with no more of this shilly-shallying, no more letting his precious girl fall into these ridiculous scrapes. With a warm, protective glow, he settled down to wait for her.

His only regret, now that the decision had been made, was that he didn't have the ring to give her, the family heirloom diamond that was given to each Wrenthe bride on her engagement. Not that he'd done it before, of course, but Wrenthe did not believe you offered for a lady without a ring on hand. It would look like a spur-of-the-moment decision, which this was, admittedly, or impetuous calf love, which no one could accuse Wrenthe of. But the ring was in the vault at Wrenthe Hall in Wiltshire. By the time he'd sent for it, had it brought back and cleaned—No, he'd have to go for it himself.

It was not fair to entrust such an item, or secret, to anyone else. In addition, he could go faster himself, riding cross-country, than a groom or even James, with the guard he would feel necessary. That he could give Noelle a different ring, one of his mother's, perhaps, or one newly purchased, was not to be considered. When a man took such a step—for the first and last time of his life, he prayed—no trumpery thing would do. It was the weight of centuries he wanted behind his suit, and that many-carated diamond in his hand. He would just have to delay the proposal.

For all Wrenthe's sense of the dignity of the occasion, he refused to ask Winston's permission to pay his addresses. It might be proper, but he'd be damned before he'd lay his heart out for some young pup. Taylor had signified his approval, anyway. Deuced irregular, mind, but Noelle wouldn't care, not his darling Nell. . . .

Noelle was still trying to scrub Sam's blood off her hands. Moira was laying out a clean gown, a pale-green dotted cambric, with trembling hands.

"Oh Miss Noelle, do you really think so? Sam'll really look at me now?"

"Only if we hurry before his eye swells shut! Come help me with the buttons, then I can manage for myself. There, now pinch your cheeks for a little colour and go on. Remember, this is your chance, girl, if you really want him!"

"Oh yes, ma'am, I do!" And she ran off.

Noelle sat at her dressing table for a moment, brushing her curls. Was this her chance? Had she been wrong, or had Wrenthe really called her darling? He must have been overcome by the scene, that was all; it was Ferne he admired.

She pinched her cheeks too, just in case.

=15=

LOVE AT FIRST BITE

WHAT A DAY it was for excitement! While Noelle was merrily recounting the kitchen episode to the Earl's warm reception, with due respect for Sam's battered face and feelings, Ferne was having an adventure of her own. Just when Noelle was sharing her amusement about Taylor's little pigeon, receiving a very melting smile in return, Ferne was setting out for home from the Kingsleys' house. Her visit to Clarice had not been pleasant, with the other girl in a pettish mood. Clarice was an active young woman who had been housebound for months; she was bored and irritable, and rightfully so, she felt. It was the most gorgeous spring day, just begging for a girl to go pick wild flowers or take a walk in the park, but the doctor would not permit it. James Waverly had called and invited her to go for a carriage ride, a very slow one, of course, but her mother would not permit *that*. The groom did not matter, nor her maid's volunteering to go along; she was not Out. Out? Why, some of those girls in their first Season, the Season that was to have been hers, were already announcing their engagements! The Kingsleys were starting to pack for the family's removal to Dorset; James was starting to plan his itinerary, travelling to his cousin's various estates. He would not wait for next year, Clarice fretted. He would forget her over the summer.

To complete her misery, Ferne had not even come by for days, to hear Clarice's woes. Miss Armstrong was too busy preparing for her party, then recuperating from it. She was too busy having fun while her poor friend suffered all alone.

Ferne tried to explain about all the callers paying their duty visits after the party, and the engagement for tea yesterday. She tried to set Dorset on the way to one or another of the Earl's properties . . . he had so many, one was bound to be close. Or else James could just come visit, if her parents would invite him. Ferne was sure Wrenthe would give him the time, because Lord Justin was such a nice man, not starchy at all, as she had first thought. Didn't he treat Ferne just like a favourite sister, when everyone knew she was a penniless nobody with hardly two thoughts to rub together?

Still Clarice remained in the doldrums, refusing to budge even when Ferne put Jasmine through her "party tricks": standing on her hind legs, rolling over, racing to her mistress when Clarice reluctantly ordered, "Find Ferne."

Ferne even tried to convince her friend that the quality of the air was poor today, that Clarice would not enjoy the park in the least; but Miss Kingsley was unhappy, and she was determined to stay unhappy until life stopped being so unfair.

Ferne decided to leave soon after tea, without waiting for Sam to return for her. She also declined the offer of a carriage from her hostess, saying, "No, thank you, I would much rather walk."

"What, in the unhealthy air?" Clarice taunted.

"Peagoose. Go bury your nose in Mrs. Radcliffe's new novel; I'll see you tomorrow."

With Jasmine on a leash at her side and the maid Janie skipping along a few feet behind, they made a lovely springtime picture. The promise of a long walk pleased Ferne, who was a country girl after all. Janie was eager too, not having her fill of the city's doings yet. It was Jasmine, the dog, who had enough of this exercise after two blocks. Being so low to the ground, her legs had to work too hard to keep it up for long. She kept sitting down until Ferne decided it was easier to carry her. The dog only weighed three or four pounds, so it was no hardship, she told Janie, who offered to carry this package like the ones she toted when her ladies went shopping.

They walked at a faster pace now, Janie nearer Ferne's side talking and laughing about the sights: the fat old man waiting for a hackney; the girl selling nosegays of violets; the shops and houses and street sweepers. So intrigued were the girls that they didn't hear any odd noises under the sounds of carriages and crowds, but Jasmine did. She leaped out of Ferne's arms, caught her balance on the pavement and took off down the alley they were just passing, her leather lead trailing behind. After the first instant's shock, the two girls were right behind her, calling her name. Jasmine did not even look over her shoulder. Ferne could hear the noises then, the snarling, snapping, gnarling of a dogfight. She called louder, ran faster in an attempt to step on the leash, but the little dog was too far ahead. There, just where the alley opened into another, narrower street that looked deserted, two huge mangy curs were trying to tear each other apart. Ferne's screams frightened off one of the mongrels but the other, a bare-patched, mud-coloured beast, turned to face its new enemy . . . a four-pound ball of white fluff, yipping and skittering about. The big dog snapped and got a mouthful of fur. Ferne was in the battle by this time, still shouting, still grabbing for the leash. Janie had her hands over her ears, but was screaming to Ferne to come away, before she too got savaged.

Ferne finally managed to step on Jasmine's trailing leash, but this was the smaller dog's undoing. Before Ferne could snatch her up and out of harm's way, most likely getting bitten herself, the enraged mutt made a lunge for its tiny adversary. Unable to dart out of the way, Jasmine was caught in two iron jaws. Horrified, shrieking hysterically, Ferne was trying to beat the dog off with her reticule, the only weapon she had. The cur only turned its head away, ready to shake the dangling Jasmine like a rat, breaking her back. Suddenly a walking stick came down solidly across the beast's muzzle. Yelping in pain, the alley dog dropped Jasmine. Then it took a hesitant step towards this latest challenger, saw the cane still raised, and slinked off through some crates.

Ferne was on the ground clutching Jasmine, who was still lying where she'd been dropped, when she felt strong fingers pry hers loose.

"There now, miss, let me take a look." It was a quiet, cultured voice that reassured her as his competent hands felt all over Jasmine.

"There's no blood, miss, and I don't feel any broken bones. Let us see if the poor mite can stand." Still kneeling beside Ferne and the fallen pup, he took his hands away.

Jasmine whimpered, then wriggled. She got her legs under her and stood, shaking herself off. And she growled.

Quickly getting a firm hold on the leash, the rescuer chuckled, a wonderful, deep, rolling sound. "Definitely more hair than wit, little furball. But no more battles for today." He handed the lead to Janie, who clutched it as if it were her last hold to earth. Then he put an arm under Ferne's elbow and raised her to her feet.

Concerned, he asked, "Are you all right, miss? That dog didn't bite you, did it?" Ferne was still staring at Jasmine, reliving the horrid nightmare of the moment she thought her dog would be killed. She only shook her head.

"I realise you must be upset, but you were very brave. Most young ladies would have fainted. . . . Shall I call a hackney for you?"

Ferne meant to thank him and say yes, please. She really did. When she finally raised her head, however, to look at her rescuer, she saw such a handsome, tanned, wholesome face, with such a kindly, caring expression, that she crumbled. From relief, guilt, sheer trauma, whatever, Ferne collapsed into the stranger's arms, sobbing. He folded her closer to his chest, patted her back and told her, "There, little kitten, it's all right." When the sobs turned to quieter weeping, he directed her to cry all she wanted, not to worry about his neckcloth. He had only spent an hour tying it, anyway. At that he received a watery giggle and felt it safe—but sorry—to take his hands away to reach for his handkerchief. He handed it to his distressed damsel, waiting for her to snuffle into it before he felt he'd better introduce himself.

"I am Sir Adam Holmes, miss, of Bedford, at your service, and . . . and delighted to have been of some use." His brain staggered as he got his first real sight of Ferne's face, reddish nose, straying curls and all.

"And . . . and I am Ferne Armstrong of . . . of Chauncey Square and Derbyshire. And I'm terribly sorry about your neckcloth and everything. I'll never be able to thank you enough for what you did and . . . and you were wonderful!''

That angel's face and pure sweet voice, as the saying went, tipped him a leveller. For Adam, it was as if he'd been a stranger travelling in a foreign country all his life, and suddenly someone called his name.

To Ferne, he was Sir Galahad and St. George—all that was kind, brave, strong and wise. The smile he was smiling at her, open and loving, offered something she'd never wanted from the boys she danced with. It was like hearing a symphony for the first time, a symphony that matched exactly the song in her heart.

She held out her hand and he kissed it. Their eyes never left each other's.

They might have stayed like that till doomsday, had not Janie recalled them to the present. ''Miss Ferne, we oughtn't be standin' in some dirty alley like this. Miss Noelle will be a-worryin'.''

''How foolish of me.'' Sir Adam, his feet on solid ground once more, finally released Ferne's hand. ''Your family will be frantic. Do you have a carriage nearby?''

''No, Sir Adam, we were walking. It was such a lovely day. Do you think you might call us that hackney? I'm afraid I'm unfamiliar with this street and . . . and would not wish to walk back through that alleyway.''

''Of course not, Miss Ferne, I would be honored to escort you home, if I may?''

''Oh yes, please.'' She blushed. ''That is, I'm sure Nellie will want to meet you, to thank you properly.''

''Nellie?''

''My sister Noelle. She was born on Christmas Day. I have a brother Winston, too, and an Aunt Hattie. They will all want to . . . to show their gratitude.''

''It will be my pleasure.''

It was bad enough having to ask Elvira Colter to send a groom to Chauncey Square for the carriage, that fool Sam forgetting to tell anyone to pick her up. Aunt Hattie would have accepted

Elvira's offer of her own coach, but she strongly suspected Mrs. Colter of cheating at cards. She refused to be beholden to such a loose fish. But then, of all the indignities, Win had come to fetch her, in his curricle! Those things were not meant for ladies of a certain age or disposition. Giving her a cheeky grin, Win handed her up to the most precarious perch ever, uncovering an indecent amount of still-trim ankle for the Colter butler to ogle in the effort. They were off to gather Ferne next, Win advised her, though where the muttonhead thought he'd seat Ferne, Janie and the dog was beyond her. Her eyes scrunched shut, the ride to Portman Square seemed shorter than she would have thought possible, longer than she would have thought she could hold her breath. She wished for her vinaigrette, but was clutching the seat rail too fiercely to search in her reticule. How every young man in London didn't end with a broken neck was a miracle! How their mothers must worry! Of course nobody's *mother* was forced to ride in such a devil's contraption, only poor aunts. And to find Ferne had left the Kingsleys'! That foolish girl, out in the London streets with a young maid and a music-box dog to protect her from the sins of the city. It was enough to give a woman palpitations! She took another sip of the sherry the Earl had considerably poured for her.

That was another thing! Hattie'd come home, barely alive, to find her younger niece unarrived and her elder alone in the front parlour with a man! What if Elvira Colter had driven her home and stopped in for tea? Noelle's reputation would be in shreds. He may be an Earl, but that did not give him the right to take liberties. Her maid should have been with them, or the butler, at least.

"What was Taylor thinking of to let this family grow so . . . so lax?" she asked the world at large. Noelle and the Earl shared a smile, neither about to reveal Taylor's distractions. "Nothing havey-cavey going on, is there, Noelle? You know how those things upset me," she said suspiciously.

"Oh no, Aunt, it's just that Sam's accident disordered the household, as I told you."

"And your maid too, miss?"

Noelle tried to look contrite. "I'm sorry, Aunt Hattie. I just wasn't thinking . . ."

"You never do, Nellie, more's the pity."

The Earl choked down a laugh. "Come now, Mrs. Deighton," he cajoled, "no harm is done, and I believe I hear a carriage now. It must be the Viscount, with Miss Ferne."

Aunt Hattie hopped up to see for herself. Her "Oh, gracious, what now?" drew the others to the window.

It was Ferne certainly, but not in Winston's smart rig. Out of a paint-peeled old carriage stepped Janie, her face as white as the little lace cap she wore, and Ferne, her hair dishevelled, her bonnet askew. The hem of her gown was inches-deep soiled, and there was mud over the bodice and skirt, where the grimy, matted dog in her arms had left footprints. The man paying the cab's jarvey was not Winston either. He was taller, stockier, more tanned and older, and received a smile from Ferne that no brother ever rated.

Noelle was first in the hall, Aunt Hattie stopping for another sip of restorative. The Earl strolled along after them, lingering in the doorway close enough to hear and be of assistance, far enough not to intrude, if it was a delicate situation.

Ferne rushed into her sister's arms, effectively destroying Noelle's second outfit of the day. Janie simply stood there, her mouth open. The stranger seemed not at all daunted or embarrassed; he just waited for Ferne to introduce him, which she did in such a jumbled fashion Noelle only gained the facts that there had been a dogfight, this gentleman had saved Jasmine from certain death, and Ferne had invited him to take potluck with them. Noelle was dismayed, not at the dogfight, which must have been terrifying, admittedly, but that Ferne was still bringing home strays to feed. Of course they owed this man a debt of gratitude, but who was he? He was dressed well enough, though not in the height of fashion, even allowing for the afternoon's exploits.

Her consternation must have been obvious as, after slightly more proper introductions, she invited Sir Holmes to return to the parlor with them while Ferne changed her gown. It was the Earl who noticed and casually asked, "That wouldn't be the Bedfordshire Holmeses, would it?"

"Why yes, the old Duke is my uncle."

Still on the staircase as if reluctant to leave Adam's presence,

Ferne exclaimed, "You didn't tell me your uncle was a duke!"

"And you didn't tell me there would be an earl here inquiring into my pedigree."

Noelle blushed as Ferne giggled on her way up the stairs. The Earl merely offered Sir Adam a glass when they were all seated. Still perfectly at ease, relaxing instantly in the stuffed, high-backed chair, his legs crossed, Adam said, "I don't want you to think I am in line for the title or anything, Miss Armstrong, Mrs. Deighton. My uncle has two sons with promising families of their own." He nodded to the Earl's speculative look before continuing. "For coming from the cavalier branch, I do respectably enough, a thousand acres or so prime farmland."

"Are you in London for a visit, Sir Adam?" Aunt Hattie asked politely.

"No, ma'am, business. I have to see about some investments. Childs' Bank handles my affairs, but I like to see to my own interests now and again." He and the Earl shared a significant pause. "I keep rooms at the Albany so I don't have to put up at a hotel."

"Surprised I haven't seen you around Town before, then. Do you go to any of the clubs?" the Earl wanted to know.

"No, I am not one for gambling, Earl; I never cared much for social goings-on either . . . before."

Noelle was growing more and more embarrassed as this not-so-subtle inquisition of Sir Adam continued. He had rescued Ferne for them; that should be enough. Of course, finding out he was of respectable birth, quite warm in the pocket in fact, was not to be sneezed at, but not quite polite either. There was something about the Earl's conversation with him, moreover, that reminded her of two male dogs sniffing around each other. She tried to apologise.

"I . . . I am sorry if we seem rudely curious, Sir Adam. It's just that Ferne is . . . That is, we . . ."

"Don't worry, Miss Armstrong, I understand. I wouldn't want any Mr. Nobody from Nowhere sharing my dinner either. And if I had a jewel like Miss Ferne, I'd make dashed certain of any man I let guard it." He shot a challenging glance at the Earl, who smiled back, nodding.

The two men seemed to have worked something out to their satisfaction, Noelle realised; she only wished she understood it. Sir Adam's intentions were quite obviously honourable, and quite honourably obvious! He was a man who liked all his cards on the table, that was for sure, but what about Wrenthe? He still wore that amiable smile that made it so hard to gauge his true feelings.

After Ferne rejoined them, radiant in a blue dimity gown, her hair brushed to a shine and caught back simply in a blue ribbon, the waters grew even more muddy. Her retelling of the dogfight and rescue was punctuated by frequent smiles and blushes and glances towards Adam for corroboration. Noelle would have to be a fool not to see that a great deal more had occurred, yet the Earl remained benignly pleasant. When Noelle had enjoyed her dancing partners, he called her a flirt; when Ferne made positive calf eyes at the man she'd just met, Wrenthe sat smiling like a cat in the cream pot. Noelle wished for an interpreter!

Dinner was a merry affair. Wrenthe cancelled an engagement with three Tory members to accept Noelle's invitation to the impromptu gathering. Winston was delighted to have male company for a change, expressing his views of petticoat tyranny to the older men, who only laughed. Win had to have the dogfight retold twice.

"Devil take it if you don't get yourself in the most harum-scarum hobbles, Ferne."

Sir Adam came to her rescue yet again: "I assure you this episode was not of Miss Ferne's making."

They all laughed when, simultaneously, the Earl and Win said, "They never are!"

When the ladies withdrew after dinner, the feeling of camaraderie prevailed, extending to first names. Win was excited to find two men so knowledgeable about the land, right under his roof. Although Wrenthe's understanding was more academic than the others', he could still join intelligently in their conversation, just as Win, and Adam more so, could discuss the House of Lords, when Wrenthe asked if Winston intended taking his seat. Winston reluctantly admitted they'd better rejoin the ladies, else his head would be on a platter. He couldn't remember when he'd had such pleasant company.

In the Chinese room, Noelle was working at a tambour frame while Aunt Hattie, as usual, was busy with her knitting. Ferne was seated at the pianoforte, practising one of the latest waltz tunes. Wrenthe took a seat next to Noelle and Adam was crossing to share Ferne's bench when he stopped suddenly, just catching sight of Jasmine and Plato. The little female had been hurriedly towelled off and brushed out before dinner, but she must have retained some scent of the attacker, for Plato was still whuffling around her, ready to do battle.

"Gads, there's another one!" exclaimed Adam. "I never saw the like and now here's a twin. Don't tell me someone's busy producing the little bleaters," he teased, having heard all about the Maltese breed on the ride home with Ferne.

"You'll get used to them," the Earl drawled. "They show up everywhere. I even have one that whines to share my bed."

"You, Justin?" Adam was disbelieving, thinking he'd misjudged his man. Everyone else laughed.

"It's my mother's really, but the blood—the blasted thing seems to prefer my company. I never met such an animal for having a mind of its own."

"And do you let it share your bed?" They all wanted to know, but Adam was the first one who dared to ask.

"No, the bed is too high for the mutt to negotiate. Besides, it has a bed of its own, with a satin coverlet, no less. I can't swear to it, but I have a strong suspicion that Jordan, my valet, uses the warming pan on the dog's bed as well as mine. Meanwhile, he keeps threatening to leave me because it is demeaning to work for a master who shares his bedroom with a lapdog."

"Why don't you toss it out?"

"Have you ever heard a wolf howl, Adam? That's what the miserable whelp sounds like when it's unhappy. Keeps the whole house awake, maids start screaming, the Countess gets the headache. No, it is easier to give in." Softening, he added, "And I told you, they grow on you," giving Noelle a special look.

After the tea tray had been brought in, Aunt Hattie coyly asked if Sir Adam, by any chance, happened to play piquet.

156

Win's snicker gave it away, so the Earl explained how Mrs. Deighton was a wizard with the pasteboards; Adam had better visit his exchequers before playing with her.

Adam laughingly took that as an excuse to decline and take his leave, promising a match soon. As he said, he did not want to wear out his welcome, not the very first day. The Earl rose to his feet also, explaining that he was off for Wiltshire the next day on family business and had preparations to see to. He would be back in time for his mother's gala, naturally, to which he cordially issued Adam an invitation, which was instantly accepted.

Noelle did not see how her sister could prefer Sir Adam Holmes's ruddy good looks and rugged, easy ways to the Earl's elegance and charm, but it was obvious that Ferne did. Not that Noelle had anything against Adam; she thought he was a fine man, in fact, steady and wholesome as an oak, and head over heels in love with Ferne. The two had smelled of April and May all evening, had shared one of the longest farewell handshakes Noelle had ever witnessed. Upstairs, it had taken forty yawning minutes before Ferne was convinced that her sister recognized Sir Adam's virtues, finally floating off to her own bedroom swearing she wouldn't sleep a wink all night.

It was Noelle who was awake hours later, though, trying to make sense of her own emotions. The Earl had been so tender towards her, so attuned to her that afternoon, sharing her amusement, then standing like a shield at her side when Ferne came home in a hired coach. And he truly did not seem to mind about Ferne and Adam. He could not have missed what was between them; his dark stare missed nothing, she was sure, even when he appeared so casually pleasant. Did it mean there was hope for her dreams after all? Now he was going away, drat the man, and she wouldn't know for a week or more if he even thought about her! She doubted if she would think of anything else!

A great many other people were also wondering about the Earl's thoughts on various matters that week.

Sir Adam Holmes became a fixture at Ferne's side, making no effort to conclude his business transactions. He could be found at Chauncey Square, in the park, at any party Miss Armstrong attended. He was never permitted more than two dances, but Ferne managed to sit out a few extra sets, Holmes nearby. The *ton* grew accustomed to this latest *affaire*. It was obviously a love match—one had only to see the couple a moment—and the family seemed to approve. It was a very respectable *parti* for the dowerless Miss Armstrong, the gossip went, but a shame when the brilliant match had been so close. And what about the Earl? Had he left town brokenhearted in the face of such a loss . . . or didn't he care? Many gentlemen with bets on at White's would give a pretty penny to find out.

Another man, no gentleman at all, had an even higher stake riding on Justin Wrenthe's involvement: Sir Rupert Dynhoff.

To his credit, the first time Dynhoff had seen Ferne in the park he had had honourable intentions. Of course he thought at the time that she was an heiress, from her chatter about Aunt Sylvia's legacy, an heiress, furthermore, whose family was so skitter-witted they let her go about unattended with Wrenthe. If they were that green, they might even permit Dynhoff to pay his addresses. He quickly learned he was wrong on both counts, but put his singularly foul interpretation on the evidence: No man as high-in-the-instep as Wrenthe would marry a penniless nobody with an uncertain reputation; therefore the Earl was desirous of setting her up as his mistress, and the family was foolishly holding out for the main chance, marriage. It was obvious. One day Wrenthe had Maringa Polieri in the phaeton in the park, the next day Miss Armstrong. Shortly after, Wrenthe broke with his Italian high-flyer and was seen squiring the new beauty around. To Dynhoff's warped experience, a man did not exchange a mistress for a wife. What for? No, a man only traded one mistress for another; wives had nothing to do with it.

So Dynhoff saw Ferne as a ladybird, unfledged as yet, but started on the garden path, and Dynhoff wanted her. Something about her innocence and purity attracted him, and the more she put him off, the greater the desire. For men of Dynhoff's cut, what they wanted, they took. He would have acted long ago, were it not for Wrenthe, one of the few men he feared. Dynhoff had no qualms about the bossy, managing sister nor the unlicked bumpkin of a brother, but while Justin

Wrenthe was interested, Dynhoff was content to stand back. He satisfied himself with anonymous efforts to sidetrack his rival, thus the tip to the Revenue Office. Certain very strong rumours had reached Dynhoff's ears, rumours worth repeating in the proper places. If by chance those rubbishing Armstrongs were found to be even vaguely connected with a smuggling operation, they would be ostracised by Society, by Wrenthe for sure. The Earl was too fastidious, too conscious of his rank and his political obligations, to handle tainted goods. That was what Miss Ferne would be, all right, with dragoons in the house, contraband in the cellars. She would not go to gaol, of course; Dynhoff would testify on her behalf if he had to, or cash in his chips with Prinny, to intercede on her behalf. And how grateful she would be!

Deuce take that plan. Nothing had been found and the Armstrongs were even more firmly entrenched in the polite world. Dynhoff decided he'd have to wait for the end of the Season. When everyone left for their summer places, the shrewish sister would see she'd been holding out for nothing; Wrenthe would never come up to scratch. Everyone knew they couldn't afford another Season for the girl, so she would have to take Dynhoff's terms. He would even make it as attractive an offer of carte blanche as he could afford: no publicity, a quiet house in Chelsea. What were a few promises? He didn't expect the sister to like it; he didn't care. He might even enjoy humbling Noelle in the process. If there was too much trouble, he had other alternatives, like taking the girl right out from under their noses, which also had its appeal. The family would squawk, but not too loudly, since no one wanted such shame spread abroad. There would be hardly anyone left in Town to hear their outrage anyway, in just a few short weeks. Dynhoff had decided he could afford to wait.

Then Adam Holmes had entered the play, changing the scenery and, inevitably, the plot. Quite plainly, Ferne and Holmes were infatuated—even one whose tastes were so jaded could recognize the fact—and the family seemed complacent, so an engagement would be coming soon. Within hours after the first public appearance of Ferne and her beau, bets had been placed at the clubs as to how soon it would be. Dynhoff barely gave Holmes a second thought. He could outshoot any country gapeseed, and what would a farmer know of fencing? Dynhoff practised with the great Frazzeti, when he could afford the Master. No, there was only one sword arm he truly feared, one pistol shot he knew he could not match. The question again came back to the Earl, who could see Dynhoff barred from Society, if he didn't kill him outright. Was Wrenthe still interested in the Rosebud? Unfortunately, Wrenthe was out of town, so there was no judging his attitude towards Ferne or Holmes. If Sir Adam found himself looking down the barrel of a pistol, or warned off, Dynhoff would bide some more; if the Earl resumed that damned negligent pose of polite disinterest, Dynhoff would have to act quickly, before Holmes carried the girl off to raise hogs.

The Countess's ball was the weathervane; half the *ton* would be watching to see how the wind blew. Ordinarily Dynhoff could not hope for an invitation from Lady Wrenthe, his reputation not meeting her high standards. That he was accepted in Society at all was due to his family name and his association with the Prince. In that circle, it was enough that Dynhoff did not beat his horses and did not cheat at cards, either of which would have seen him banned from his clubs, separated from his livelihood of gaming. A man's morals didn't matter so much over the green baize tables, and he was a haloed saint compared to some of the royal family. Most likely they would not be invited to Wrenthe House either. In this instance, there was an easy way to get an invitation: A few lucky rolls of the dice, a note slipped to a certain jockey and Dynhoff had enough to send a cheque to the Countess for her damned orphans. A waste of good blunt, he thought, but hell, some of the bastards might even be his.

If Dynhoff could have seen Lady Wrenthe's grimace of distaste as she wrote out the invitation to him, he would only have relished it more. He moved ahead with his plans.

=16=

THE BEST-LAID PLANS

NOELLE HAD SEEN Wrenthe House, Grosvenor Square, before. She had seen the Earl's study on one memorable occasion, a formal drawing room on another, and a sunny, cosy parlour where the Countess served tea. Nothing had prepared her for this. By day the entrance hall was a vast dark cavern tiled in black and white marble, echoing with the footsteps of a hundred dead Wrenthes, their portraits lining the walls along both sides of the massive double-arched stairways. Tonight the balustrades were twined with flowers, creating a bower effect, and so many guests filled the hall and the stairs, waiting to reach the receiving line at the top, that no one could have seen the mosaics on the floor. It was already a grand squeeze, obviously a success, and the whole thing was brilliantly lighted.

"Lord Justin has those new gas lamps," Ferne exclaimed, awed. "And they don't even smoke."

Adam laughed as Win said "They wouldn't dare."

Then it was the Armstrongs' turn to greet their host and hostess. The Countess was stunning, a diamond tiara on her white hair, but it was Wrenthe who stole Noelle's breath. She had thought he could never look more magnificent than he had that first night at Almack's, in the required formal evening clothes, yet tonight he did—tonight he was smiling, just for her. She was sure of it. After he'd signed his name to her dance card twice, she floated on to the reception rooms. The Earl patted his waistcoat pocket much as if he were touching a good-luck piece, before offering his hand to the next guest.

One room just past the receiving line was used to display the results of Aunt Hattie and her friends' efforts, the way gifts would be arrayed at a wedding. Piled on tables, draped over chairs, dangling from a cord stretched between two wall sconces, were hats, mitts, scarves, sweaters and shawls—enough to keep King Richard's Children's Army warm on their way to the Crusades. Some of the children might find one sleeve longer than another, odd loops here and there on a hat, a glove missing a finger, but the ladies had tried. Considering that knitting was a plebian skill, previously shunned by the upper classes, who preferred to see their women doing silk embroidery or knotting a fringe or beading a reticule, the women under Hattie's direction had done remarkably well. Her already ample bosom swelled with pride as everyone praised the work.

Moving toward the ballroom doors, Noelle was stunned again. Compared to this, the Chauncey Square room she'd thought so splendid was like something seen through the wrong end of Galileo's telescope! Whatever could they use this place for, when not entertaining on such a grand scale? Winnie thought it would make an excellent riding academy, mirrored as it was, except for the problem of getting the horses up the stairs. Giggling, Ferne guessed they could let water freeze on it for a skating pond. It was Adam who reminded them that people as well-heeled as Wrenthe did not have to worry about such things as heating an unused barrack of a place, finding furniture for it or paying servants to clean it. After all, Wrenthe had at least three other houses, almost unoccupied. What was a ballroom or two? This all took Noelle by surprise. Somehow she'd forgotten how very wealthy the Earl was. She'd known he was one of the warmest men in England, as rich as Golden Ball, they said. It was one of the things that had pleased her, for Ferne's sake. Now doubts began to nibble away some of the glow she had been warming her heart on. Their circumstances were so different . . . he could have any girl, anywhere. Devil take it, she would *not* let such thoughts ruin her evening, not when there were acres of flowers and oceans of champagne adding their heady excitement to the convention of butterflies milling about. There were over two hundred people in their fanciest dress, with at least another hundred waiting for their carriages to get close enough to discharge them onto the red carpet. It was rumoured that the Prince himself would attend, although the Countess was disdainful.

"He'll make an appearance—he loves it when everyone has to stop what they are doing to bow—and he'll promise me a cheque for the children. I am still waiting for his last promise. The man owes everyone money. Parliament will have to pay his debts again, so what's another pledge from him? Useless parasite, that's what he is, and fat as a flawn, too. At least he'll give the ball the final touch; royalty always does, with these snobs."

Noelle couldn't help it, old reprobate or not, she was eager to meet "the first Gentleman of Europe." If that made her a snob, she was in excellent company.

The Earl found himself in a quandary. He was host to over three hundred people and he only wanted to be near one of them, Noelle. That he was throwing such a bash at all was half a surprise to him; he'd been consulted as much as he'd been about the choice of his middle name. He was host only in that he happened to own the house and was, without a doubt, footing the bills for his mother's extravaganza. Just like her to see her charities prosper and her son in the poorhouse, he thought ruefully. Not that he minded, except that being host entailed a great many obligations. Standing on the receiving line for over an hour, for instance, when he'd wanted to quit it at the Armstrongs' arrival. Or having to open the dancing with a Russian princess, and follow with a duchess, when he only wanted to have one green-eyed witch in his arms. He knew he couldn't dance solely with Noelle, of course. Singling her out in such a fashion would be tantamount to a notice in the *Gazette*, and what if she refused him later? No, he would do his duty for the first half of the evening, at least. He'd put himself down on Noelle's card for the supper dance, hoping that perhaps there would be a moment of privacy. If not, he had one more dance reserved with her, to put his luck to the test. He'd ask her to sit it out with him, perhaps strolling on the balcony. It was not quite proper, which would not faze his Nell in the least, if she wanted to be alone with him. It was a big *if*. One way or another, the night should put him out of this misery of indecision. Such were Wrenthe's plans.

Adam signed Ferne's card for the first dance and the supper dance, then both he and Ferne turned pleading eyes to Noelle.

Smiling, she nodded and Holmes wrote in a third for later. It could not make a farthing's difference, Noelle reasoned; anyone with two eyes could see it had been love at first sight between them. Having a wide streak of romanticism colouring her own viewpoint, she could only sigh: the beautiful maiden saved by the dashing hero just in the nick of time (for poor Jasmine, anyway). It only remained to say they lived happily ever after; Noelle expected to hear an announcement about that shortly. Beside his three dances with Ferne and one with Noelle, Adam was expecting Winston to introduce him to some gentlemen familiar with Coke's agricultural experiments. Those were Adam's intentions for the evening.

Sir Rupert Dynhoff put his own plans into operation before the first set. Bowing over Ferne's hand, he opened her dance book before she could say it was filled. What he saw there delighted him: three sets with the Provincial, none with Wrenthe. So the Earl had tired of the game and retired from the lists, well, well. Dynhoff put his own name down for a dance after supper, when the aunt would be in the card room and his chances for getting Miss Ferne away from that harpy of a sister were better. Yes, his plans were coming along nicely.

Ferne did not care whom she danced with, if it could not be Adam, but she shivered a little. Something about Dynhoff made her cold, or perhaps she was just too close to the windows. She moved nearer to Adam to wait for the dancing to begin. Noelle frowned at Dynhoff's back, fully intending to speak to Ferne about it later, reminding her not to leave the ballroom with Sir Rupert, not for an instant. There was nothing she could do about it now, with her own partner coming to claim her for the dance.

That was how the first half of the evening passed: Noelle and Dynhoff both watching Ferne, and both curious to see whom the Earl danced with, though for very different reasons.

The supper laid out for the Countess's three hundred plus guests could have fed the orphans for a year, but no one commented on the discrepancy as they gorged themselves on stuffed prawn and syllabub, spun-sugar baskets filled with fruits from Wrenthe's succession houses. The Earl found that the greatest delicacy was the dimpled smile Noelle was serving him, but there was no time for him to make his declaration and taste that particular sweet. By the time they had had their fill, the orchestra was retuning for the next set. Wrenthe did think of delaying the music for a while, whimsically deciding that since he was paying the piper, he could also pay him *not* to play. He discarded the notion as unworthy, besides being impractical. How could he propose while three hundred people waited for the music? He would wait until the later dance, after all.

His decision went for nothing. The orchestra struck up a tune, faltered and petered out to silence. Everyone murmured about the explanation, then they turned to the doorway to see it, or him. George, Prince of Wales and Regent for his father the mad King, had arrived and was filling an inordinate amount of the entrance with his red-faced girth. Nor did he come alone; Petersham, Alvanley, Brummell, even Freddy Byng tagged along in his wake. A dissolute, debauched and indiscreet old roué he might be, but he was still the Prince. He was loved by few and respected by less, even those who were fond of him admitting his incompetence as a ruler. An immoral extravagance, was how the caricaturists depicted him, caring more for his pleasures than for his people. For all of that, the ladies bobbed and blushed, the men bowed and stammered when he shook their hands, waving negligently for the orchestra to begin anew, very much as though *he* were host.

Wrenthe grinned. For all that Prinny was a damned nuisance to Parliament, an old fool when it came to his love life, the Earl liked him, liked his charm and style and enjoyment of life. He stepped forward to greet his Prince, making his most elegant leg, then shaking the sovereign's hand when it was offered.

Prinny was delighted with the party, his reception and the Countess's good work. ("I'll have my exchequer see about it in the morning." The Countess curtsied but smirked.) In general, he did not stay long at any social function, accepting his obsequies and then quickly growing bored. Tonight, however, the Prince was in a congenial mood. He seemed to wish to spend time with these people, the few who could be counted on not to boo him in the streets, before they left Town. His arm on

Wrenthe's shoulder, he made the rounds of the ballroom, laughing here, pinching a debutante's cheek there, clapping a man on the back in great good spirits. It was better than squiring another titled lady around the floor, so Wrenthe did not mind, until the Prince recalled hearing of two new stars in the social skies, old Sterling's gals.

"Now there was a man," the Prince declared. "Wish there were more like him today, instead of the damned lily-livered macaronis we've got. They say the younger gal's got his looks but the older's got a sparkle to her. Where are you hiding 'em, eh, Justin?"

Wrenthe did not find the Regent quite so charming when, between dances, he introduced the ladies and watched the future King lick his lips. Ferne the Prince called a delightful child, to her rosy-faced embarrassment, but Noelle he asked to dance, to Wrenthe's aggravation. The Prince was not usually attracted to young, single women, which was lucky, since he could generally be counted on to offend their virgin ears. At least, thought Wrenthe, the Prince was cutting out Millbrooke on Noelle's programme. The Prince would then depart; Wrenthe could see him to the door with all due pomp and still return in time for his own long-awaited dance.

The Prince was moist-faced and panting after his exertion, however, needing refreshment. With Noelle's arm still in his, he turned to the punch table, Wrenthe and some of the royal retinue trailing after. They all stood chatting about art, one of Prinny's great enthusiasms. The Prince described one of his recent acquisitions to Noelle, who seemed to be interested, Wrenthe noted, not at all upset to be missing her dance with Ramsey now. Wrenthe mentioned a new purchase of his, a Raphael, hoping to see if Noelle's tastes matched his, but this was a grave error on his part. The Prince wanted to see the painting. Droolly and decadent he might be, but one could still not outright refuse the future King of England.

"I am terribly sorry, Highness, but I am promised for this dance to Miss Armstrong. You wouldn't want the lady to miss the ball, would you?"

"Gammon, Justin, Byng here can keep her company.

They've got a lot in common, don't you know, both seem to be nutty about dogs." He bowed over Noelle's hand, his stays creaking. "Now where's the Raphael? You know, I've always preferred the Italian school. Alvanley here feels. . . . "

After the supper, Adam knew he had at least an hour before he could dance with Ferne again. He had no desire to see her whisk by in some other man's arms either. It was not out of jealousy, mind—he did not doubt Ferne's affections any more than he did his own—but it was frustrating all the same. The lads who surrounded her between dances were rattles, with a few lyrical halflings practising their romantic flights. It was amusing at first, then just boring. This was as good a time as any to search out Win for that talk on crop rotation, or at least step out to the balcony to blow a cloud. . . .

So it was, Noelle in the refreshment room discussing canines with Poodle Byng, Adam talking turnips with Win and a Yorkshireman, Aunt Hattie beating her opponents to flinders in the card room, and Wrenthe giving a private showing to the Prince, that Ferne was left unchaperoned during Dynhoff's dance. Nothing could happen to her anyway, not in front of three hundred guests, with the Countess nearby, could it?

Dynhoff was not so crude. Or so foolhardy. He was going to abduct Ferne, all right, and ruin her reputation so no man would ever marry her, and she would have to become his mistress, but he did not intend to steal her from under Wrenthe's nose. Personally interested or no, the Earl would not approve. For now, Dynhoff's plan basically required a little more groundwork laid, a foundation he did not wish overheard.

Ferne did not want to sit out the dance with him, much less leave the ballroom to get a glass of punch, until he told her he had some serious news to impart concerning her pets, which must remain private between them.

"My dogs? Why, you must tell me at once! There, we can stand near the opened windows. No one can hear us, and I will have kept my word to Noelle not to leave the ballroom. I can't imagine what you would want to tell me about Jasmine . . . "

"Not your own dog, Miss Armstrong, but little dogs, and big

dogs, and terrible, evil things done to them. Do you know anything about dog pits?"

"You mean the dogfights where men gamble on the outcome? My brother once told me. It was too awful!"

"Too awful by half! Yet they go on, for depraved souls to wager on the gory, bloody results. Did you know that they put two dogs in the pit and then yell and shout until the dogs tear each other apart? And if a dog refuses to fight, its master takes it out and whips it!" She was beginning to look queer so he changed his tack. "Now they are starting to use smaller dogs, bred just for strength and meanness, dogs they train by putting them against even smaller, weaker animals—like yours!"

"Oh no! It cannot be! No one could be so cruel!" Ferne was near to tears, half with the remembrance of Jasmine's brush with death, half with the horrible picture Dynhoff had just painted for her.

"It happens, I swear. That is why I need your help, why I came to you."

"Me? What could I do? I don't understand. . . ."

He leaned a little closer to her. "I have heard that there is to be a dogfight tomorrow morning, just out of town, and I intend to stop it! This evil cannot be permitted to continue!"

"Can't the magistrates do something? The constables . . ."

"All turn a deaf ear. They all get a share of the profits, which is why I have to swear you to secrecy. If they got wind of our plan, they would merely move the dogs to another location. No, someone who truly cares about animals must step in before one more innocent dog is brutalized in such a manner."

"Oh Sir Rupert, I did not realize you had such . . . such noble sentiments."

"It is what any right-thinking man would do. But I still need your help." Ferne looked up at him trustingly, eagerly. It would have melted his heart, if he had one. "You're the only person I can rely on. Most of the men here would not lift a finger to stop it. Quite the contrary, my dear, they will most of them be attending. I even heard that Holmes fellow getting directions to it from some fellow in the card room. As for the other women, none of them have your sensitivity, your understanding of dogs."

Doubtfully, remembering how ineffective she had been with her reticule and the big brown mongrel, she asked, "But what could I do? I don't think I could—"

"No, no," he interrupted. "Nothing dangerous. My plan is to create a disturbance just before the first dogs are matched. My man will be there; he'll shout 'fire' or some such, and in the confusion he and I will untie the dogs from the back room. My man can hold a pistol on the crowd if he has to. If we just set the dogs loose, however, their owners will simply recapture them, so we have to carry them away. This is where I need your help, someone with a knowledge of the animals, someone who cares about them. Please do not disappoint me, or them."

Ferne still did not understand the actual part she was to play in all this. Perhaps her job was to keep the dogs calm, or feed them tidbits so they would not bark, or something like that. She often did not understand things in their entirety, but she knew her duty when she saw it.

"Good. Can you leave your house early? Say eight? That way we will get there in time, and no one will stop you."

"Stop me? But Nellie—"

"Your sister dislikes me. I cannot blame her; a man's reputation is all she has to judge by. She would never let you go, no matter how worthy the cause. Here is my chance to prove her wrong. I will see that you come to no harm, and save a score of those poor, wretched, underfed animals."

It sounded just plausible enough to Ferne. Here too was her chance to prove to Noelle that her younger sister was grown up, old enough to know her own mind and get married soon. If Ferne could deal with this on her own, which she was sure she could, given enough mutton bones, then Noelle would have to see she wasn't quite so cabbageheaded. Ferne did not want to think about Sir Rupert's hint that Adam might be going to bet on the dogs, not her dear, gentle Adam! She would not believe that. His friends might take part, though, and he might not let Dynhoff stop the pit fight, out of loyalty, so she agreed not to tell him either. She admitted she could leave the house at eight o'clock, especially after a ball; no one would look for her until twelve, and she would be back by then.

Then Ferne added a little twist to the plan that would have

pleased Dynhoff had he known its effects on Wrenthe and Noelle. Ferne felt she needed some sleep before such a venture, so as soon as Noelle returned to the ball she claimed a terrible migraine and an urgent need for her own bed.

Aunt Hattie was fetched, Win and a concerned Adam hurriedly summoned. No one was more worried than Noelle, no one more disappointed than the Earl. He patted the waist-coat pocket again as he watched their carriage pull away.

=17=

THE ABDUCTION

"YOU CAME." DYNHOFF exhaled in relief as his man closed the carriage door on the trim brown-cloaked figure. Getting Ferne out of the house without setting off the hue and cry had been the chanciest part of his scheme. Now, Sir Rupert relaxed against the worn squabs and tapped his cane for the driver to move on, away from Chauncey Square. The man had his instructions: fast enough to put some distance between them and possible pursuit; not fast enough to attract attention. It was only eight A.M. after all.

"And you did not talk about this with anyone?"

"No. You said not to, and you were quite right, when I thought about it. Noelle would not have permitted me to come. I do think you were wrong about Adam, though. He once told me he hardly hunts because he finds it too brutal. He is much too good a man to go to dogfights."

"Maybe so, maybe so," Dynoff conceded. Lord, how he was enjoying this. His pretty little bird did not even know she was in the net.

Ferne was looking around. "I do not see any meat or bones for the dogs. You didn't forget, did you?"

He could have lied and told her the package was up by the driver, but it was time to see the bird flutter. He told her there was no meat, no bones.

"But we decided that was the best way to keep the dogs happy and quiet. They most likely starve the dogs to make them meaner and fight harder."

"My dear Miss Armstrong, there is no dogfight."

"No dogfight? Then where are we going?"

"We are going to my house in South Broome Street, for the evening."

"I don't understand. You know I cannot stay the evening with you. Please stop and let me down!"

"Rosebud, this is not a do-gooders' tea party. This is an abduction. You will be my guest whether you like it or not. Then we shall see about tomorrow."

Ferne looked out the window reflectively. "Oh" was her only comment.

" 'Oh?' That's all you have to say?"

"Well, I thought such might be the case," she said finally, calmly.

Dynhoff was taken aback. "You thought I was going to abduct you and you came anyway?"

"I felt it was my duty, just in case there was really going to be a dogfight. Nellie is always telling me a person should act in accordance with her beliefs, so I did." She sat back in her corner of the seat.

"You seem remarkably calm, little lady, for a woman who will be ruined by morning."

"Oh, I am not frightened. Noelle will never let that happen. She will yell and scream at me that I never think before I do something, but I try. Somehow I think and think, and still get the wrong answers. Mad or not, she will make sure Winnie or Adam comes for me before dark."

"You better start worrying, missy. Those two nodcocks will never find you!"

Ferne considered that. "No? Well then I suppose Justin will. . . . He must know you better."

"Wrenthe?" Dynhoff sneered, ignoring for now the second part of Ferne's statement. "What makes you think Wrenthe would come to your aid? He never puts himself out for anyone, least of all silly chits. I saw him last night; he never looked at you."

"Me? Of course not, but he would do anything Noelle asked him to."

"What?" Suddenly the game was not going his way. Dynhoff's forehead started to glisten.

"Didn't you know?" Ferne asked nonchalantly. "He is quite *épris*. Taylor had a bet the announcement will come this month, but I am not so sure."

Her abductor removed his handkerchief and wiped his face. "No matter, he'll never find you either. He would have no reason to think you were with me."

"Oh yes he would"—proudly—"I told Noelle in my note. I knew that what I was doing was right, you see, and I understood why it must be secret, but I could not stand lying to Nell or letting her find me missing if we were not back in time. I told her exactly where I was going, so she wouldn't worry."

"You fool!" Dynhoff grabbed her shoulders in a rage. "You stupid little fool!" He struck her across the face. "*Now* are you frightened?"

Ferne had been laughed at by Winnie, when she had fallen into her innumerable hobbles, and fretted over by Aunt Hattie. Mostly she had been shouted at by Noelle, who usually apologised later for her abominable temper. In Ferne's entire life she had never been struck. She still was not scared; she'd fainted dead away.

Dynhoff left her where she had slumped, thinking furiously. He had three options, as far as he could figure: He could dump Ferne out and lay low for a while, hoping that with no harm done Wrenthe would forget him. There was not much chance of that. He could flee with Ferne out of the country, to Gretna or Dover, hoping to outrace the pursuit, but the odds were not good, with this old lumbering coach. Or he could proceed as planned, take her to his town house and brazen it out . . . deny the whole thing and negotiate later, when he'd held the trump card overnight. He might have to marry the widgeon, who was a lot less appealing suddenly, or let Wrenthe pay a ransom to see him out of the country, but he might end up with his skin. Ever a gambler, Dynhoff let the carriage continue to South Broome Street.

At about the same time that Ferne was being carried, still unconscious and covered with an old blanket, through the service door of Dynhoff's seedy residence, Noelle was sitting down to breakfast. She had not slept well again, a habit acquired since meeting the Earl, and her head felt muzzy and thick. She was sipping her coffee and just nibbling the corner of her toast when Aunt Hattie bustled in.

"Is that all you are having, Noelle? Don't tell me you are sickening for something, too?"

"I'm just tired, Aunt Hattie. Too much excitement, I suppose. Did you check on Ferne? I called at her door, but got no answer so I came away. A good sleep will be the best thing for her."

"I tiptoed in but the curtains were still drawn, and I did not want to disturb her either. I told Moira to listen for her bell. Why didn't you stay abed, too?"

"Do you mean to tell me you didn't hear Win leave this morning? He was in tearing spirits, must have taken the stairs in threes. Taylor tells me he and Adam were off to Tattersall's. There is nothing Win likes better. I could not fall back to sleep, then the dogs wanted putting out, and I worried about Ferne. I think I'll check on her as soon as I've finished my coffee."

Before she had one more swallow, Taylor was in the doorway, clearing his throat. "Lady Bromley from next door has called to see you, Miss Noelle. I said you were not receiving visitors, but she, ah, said she would wait."

"Oh Nell," Aunt Hattie wailed, "whatever can that awful creature want at this time of the morning? Do say you are not taking morning calls, or *something*. You know how upsetting she was last time!"

Noelle patted her aunt's hand. How could she forget the last meeting with her formidable neighbour? Lady Bromley had tapped her way into the sitting room, then waved the cane around, threatening lamps, vases and portraits. She was in a fury over Noelle's inferior servants running amok in her kitchen. Sam, of course. Without listening to explanations or apologies, Lady Bromley expressed her opinion of her previous neighbour, Great-aunt Sylvia (poor), and her quickly formed estimation of the current household (worse). Whatever Lady Bromley wanted today, it was *not* a polite social call.

"In the front parlour, is she? I suppose I'd best go see what she wants," Noelle said reluctantly. When she saw her aunt's stricken face she smiled and added, "There is no reason both of us must have our digestions ruined. You stay here and finish your kippers, Aunt, I'll see about Lady Bromley."

The lady was not brandishing her walking stick, but was sitting erect, both hands folded on its knobbed head, a sly grin on her hag-lined face.

"It won't fadge, missy, just won't fadge," she began as soon as Noelle shut the door behind her. "You with all your airs and so-called connections. Wait to see how quickly they drop you now, you and that loose sister of yours."

Noelle had no idea what Lady Bromley was talking about, and told her so, thinking that maybe she was still dreaming.

"Don't go all hoity-toity on me, miss. It won't wash! Here you are playing the grand lady while your sister is all hugger-mugger, getting into men's carriages at eight in the morning."

Noelle was definitely dreaming—a nightmare. Gathering her composure like a shawl, Noelle announced, "I do not care for your innuendoes or inventions, my lady. You can ask anyone who attended the Countess of Wrenthe's ball last night"—an unworthy but satisfying dig; Lady Bromley had not been invited—"my sister had to leave early; she was feeling unwell. At this minute she is still abed, and we are waiting to see if the doctor should be called."

"Hogwash! I know what I saw. I've got eyes in my head, girl, and it was that little yellow-haired chit I saw meet a man at the corner. It was clear as day from my bedroom window; a brown cloak she was wearing, and a brown poke bonnet. If you think I'll keep this to myself, the more fool you are."

"I am afraid it will be you made to look the fool, ma'am," Noelle said, thinking frantically. "My sister is abed and furthermore owns no brown wrap. She certainly would not leave the house unattended at eight o'clock to meet a man. What you saw, most likely, was our maid, out to do an errand. Ferne is not the only fair-haired girl, you know."

"Then why did this 'maid' of yours meet the carriage at the corner, I'd like to know?" The look on the old gabblemonger's face was a smug dare.

Noelle answered it with a sweet smile. "Why, so the carriage wheels would not disturb your rest, of course, at such an early hour. Now if you will excuse me, I should bring poor dear Ferne the broth Cook is making up special." She pulled the bell rope. Taylor appeared so promptly he could only have been standing right outside the door, listening. "Lady Bromley was just leaving, Taylor."

"Of course, miss. This way, my lady."

The instant the front door closed behind Lady Bromley, Noelle was tearing up the stairs, skirts flying. She skidded around the landing, wrenched open Ferne's door, whooshed the bed hangings apart—and found a letter propped on the pillow. Hands trembling, she tore it open to read: "Dearest Nell, In case you find this and start to worry, please do not. I have gone on a noble mission to rescue some dogs from the pits of hell, with Sir Rupert Dynhoff, who is not as black as you have painted him. I hope. Please forgive my deception, it was a call to moral duty. I *should* be home by twelve. Love, Ferne."

It was already 10:30; Lady Bromley, the old witch, had said Ferne left at 8. She could be anywhere by now. Rushing back down the stairs, Noelle nearly collided with Sam, hurriedly summoned from the stables by Taylor who, knowing Miss Ferne, anticipated the worst. A quick whispered conference and Sam was sped off to find Win and Adam, discreetly. There was time and enough for the prattle boxes to feast on this hubble-bubble.

Aunt Hattie disintegrated at the news, despite Noelle's attempts at reassurance. Hattie was faint. She was dizzy. She needed her smelling salts, her hartshorn and water, a stiff belt of brandy.

"Just like her father," was all she could mutter. "The midwife should have drowned her at birth." When she started to wail, Noelle called for Moira to help her to bed, a cloth soaked in lavender water on her brow.

For all the lift Noelle had tried to give Aunt Hattie's spirits, she was not exactly confident herself. If it had been anyone but Dynhoff! He was such a schemer—you could tell by his red-rimmed, watery eyes—he would have made sure of his getaway.

Where would they even start to search? She prayed Win or Adam or Taylor would know. That was just the kind of thing Taylor *would* know, she decided, feeling a little better. Poor Ferne must be frightened by now, though, realizing her noble mission was a farce and she was in terrible danger. Dear, sweet Ferne, Noelle thought ruefully, remembering something her father really had said, many years ago, rescuing Ferne from some bumble bath or other. She was so pretty, he'd said, the angels kept her playing too long, when all the other babies were waiting their turn for brains.

Please, please let her be safe, Noelle prayed.

Winston and Adam burst in, Sam and Taylor right behind. Win, who had pulled Ferne out of ponds where she was "saving" an injured duck, and down from trees when she was rescuing a lost kitten, tended to treat this as just another of Ferne's hey-go-mad starts; it was a lark for him to be an avenging knight this time. He was even looking forward to finding Dynhoff and giving him what-for. Nell looked at him aghast—he was even more like Ferne than she'd realized!

Sir Adam, white-faced and tense, took matters much more seriously. It took all of their persuasiveness to keep him from tearing off after Ferne . . . and where would he start? Taylor took over, assigning Win, Adam and Sam each a section of posting houses to cover. Dynhoff's team was well known; Ferne was unmistakeable. Someone would have noticed if they passed by. Winnie took the Dover Road; Sir Adam took the inns by the Great North Road, leading to Gretna Green, just in case Dynhoff's intentions were halfway honourable, which Noelle doubted. Sam left for the road towards Reading because Taylor recalled Dynhoff's family coming from there. Sir Rupert had long ago gambled away the estate, but perhaps he had a relative in the vicinity who would assist him. Taylor himself would get over to The Duck and the Drake to see if anyone there knew of Dynhoff's activities, if he owned a hunting box, which cronies were likely to let him use their cottages, etc. Taylor would leave a trusted footman on duty at the door so things looked normal, if anyone came to call. His instructions were to inform visitors that Miss Ferne was indeed ill and the family was not receiving.

As for Noelle, her job was to wait to receive information. Each man was to report back to her, or send a message if he found a clue, so she could send the others on after.

When they had all gone, she realized she had the hardest job, with nothing to do but fret herself to flinders. She itched to go pull on her riding habit and set out *ventre à terre* after them, which would do nothing but create more scandal broth for Lady Bromley to lap up. Noelle could not just sit still, though. Pacing, she tried furiously to think of some other possibility, another explanation. Rather than answers, she only found more questions, and a lot of guilt. She had let Ferne grow away from her recently, when they had used to be so close. Even last night, Noelle had been so wrapped up in her own dreams of the Earl that she had let Moira help Ferne to bed, without going in to see how she did. Maybe Ferne would have told her then, or maybe Noelle could have noticed a glitter of excitement in Ferne's eyes. At least Noelle could have discovered Ferne's headache was a sham and been on her guard. It was all her fault! She should have watched Dynhoff more closely, not let him near innocent, unsuspecting Ferne. She should have known better. Noelle started to weep.

Wrenthe drove towards Chauncey Square whistling. It was a fine day, a beautiful day, in fact, and he was filled with confidence. His waistcoat pocket was again filled with the family ring. The way Noelle had looked at him with such regret at their missed dance, her sad backwards glance when the Armstrongs had had to leave early—he was about to become the happiest man on earth. If only Ferne stayed resting in her room and Mrs. Deighton could be convinced to leave them alone. . . .

Young Sterling drove by in his curricle, a little quickly for this traffic, typical of the nodcock, the Earl thought, raising his whip to return Win's cheerful greeting. At least one of the family was out of the house.

A man on horseback tore past, a large, well-set man, at a bruising pace. It registered on the Earl that Sir Adam Holmes was just such a hearty figure, although he had only seen the man twice, and never on horseback. Wrenthe lowered his hands until his team stepped up the pace a bit.

Then around the corner came Sam, riding hell-for-leather. There was no missing that battered face anywhere. Wrenthe put the chestnuts to a gallop.

Noelle heard the altercation in the hallway, the footman trying to keep someone out. There was a powerful low counterpoint, quiet yet forceful. Noelle could not hear what was said, but she knew who was saying it. She ran to the sitting-room door just as it was opening. The footman behind Wrenthe, arguing and apologising, had the door slammed in his face. Noelle found herself crying into Justin's shirtfront, and very satisfying it was, too.

"Shh," he soothed, rocking her slightly in his arms and, she could swear, kissing the top of her head. "Come now, Nellie darling, what's to do? Everyone's racing down the streets . . . won't you let me help?"

One more whimper, a gulp, a hand brushed across her eyes and she was almost ready to step out of the security of his arms. Reluctantly, he let her go, but held one of her hands in his while she sniffled: "It's . . . it's Ferne."

"And what else is new, dear heart?"

Ignoring the sarcasm and the endearment, tears still falling, she went on to explain, about Lady Bromley, Dynhoff, the dogs.

Wrenthe cursed, then excused himself for it. "I'm sorry, but your sister is a damned peaheaded nuisance. And I suppose you are going to blame me because I introduced them."

"How can you be so . . . so insensitive? How can you make fun at a time like this?" she stormed at him.

"Shush, Nell, I just wanted to stop your weeping so I could think." He ran his finger down her straight little nose, then kissed it, saying, "I've been wanting to do that for an age," before walking away to do some pacing of his own. Blushing, a little breathless, Noelle waited. At last he snapped his fingers.

"I have an idea," he told her, putting his arms around her waist, "but I may be wrong . . . No, I am not going to discuss it. I'll be back shortly, though." He brushed her forehead with his lips. "You realise, I hope, that I have never exerted myself so much on anyone's behalf, and you better appreciate it." She was staring at him, confused but more confident every minute—about Ferne, about him. He kissed her lips, so gently it may have been a sunbeam, so warm did it make her feel. "When we get the wretched brat home," he told her, giving her one of those special smiles, "I'll expect some reward."

===18===
EVERY DOG HAS ITS DAY

ADAM HAD RETURNED nearly frantic, with no word or sign, and been sent out again towards the Guildford Road by Taylor. When Winnie arrived home, even he was beginning to worry; he admitted he was glad that Wrenthe was also searching.

"Though why you couldn't have found where he was off to I don't know, Nell. Could have saved us a lot of tearing around the countryside. A downy one like Wrenthe, he's sure to come up a winner. I'm off for the Brighton Road. Taylor thinks it's as good a spot as any for an abduction, all those vacant houses off season."

Noelle found it easier to wait this time. Moira and she had dosed Aunt Hattie with the tiniest bit of laudanum, so Noelle was spared that moaning as she continued to pace. She tried to push the terrible ideas out of her mind, like how much time had passed and what if they found Ferne too late and Dynhoff had— No. She would think instead how Justin could do anything he set out to do. Hadn't he seen them made the toasts of the Town? He would bring Ferne home and then . . . That was much more pleasant conjecture! After a time, Noelle could even smile, wondering what Lady Bromley must be thinking of all this coming and going, after her Banbury tale about the maid. Noelle hoped her nose froze flat, from being pressed so long against the windowpane.

At last she heard another carriage drive up, Wrenthe in the hall with Taylor. The Earl walked very casually into the parlour and kissed her hand. He accepted a glass of port from Taylor, then made himself comfortable in a high-backed wing chair. Taylor was hovering near the door, reluctant to leave without any information. He cleared his throat. Noelle did not have patience for such subtleties.

"You beast! Aren't you going to tell us where you've been? Do you know where Ferne is?"

Wrenthe smiled tenderly. "Where I have been is visiting our friend Dynhoff. While your brother and Adam have been chasing their tails Dynhoff has been sitting at home. I *think* Ferne is there, but I am not certain."

"And you did not find out?" She gasped.

The Earl flicked a speck of dust off his Hessians. "My dear, I just happened to find myself in Dynhoff's neighbourhood and thought I would pop in for a brandy. Very inferior stuff too, Taylor, by the way. The butler kept me waiting until Dynhoff saw fit to receive me. I wondered if Rupert had seen your sister this morning, if he knew how she was feeling. He replied that he had taken her for a drive earlier, but she had a relapse of the headache, so he brought her home. He did not come in because his horses were too fresh."

"You did not believe him, did you?" Noelle wanted to know.

"Not in the least. His eyes would not meet mine and he seemed anxious, cordial enough but jumpy. I could not simply come out and accuse him of stashing a kidnapped virgin away in his attics, though."

"Why not?" Noelle asked. Certainly that was what she would have done.

"I was a guest in his house; it would have been exceedingly bad *ton*." Before she could tear into him, he went on: "No, without proof, I could not very well ask to search his house. He could have her anywhere, or slip her out the back. I did not want him to grow suspicious and maybe act out of desperation, so I came away."

"But my lord Wrenthe," Taylor inquired, "what if he has already spirited Miss Ferne out of London and is waiting for darkness to join her?"

"I do not think it likely, but I left my tiger across the way to see if anyone leaves the premises. I think she's still there, however. Right now, Dynhoff must be thinking he has outfoxed us, thrown us off the scent by being where we least expect him. It's better that way. He will grow more confident, let down his guard.''

Sitting calmly by without acting in a crisis was not Noelle's style. She was about to burst. ''When do we go back? Are we waiting for Win and Adam?''

'' 'We'?'' Wrenthe raised one eyebrow, then he laughed at Noelle's look of outrage. ''I am only teasing! You can come along. In fact, you will have to, for propriety's sake, if we want to scotch the rumours. It would not do for Ferne to arrive home alone with me. I do not think we need to wait for Holmes or Sterling . . . they're liable to be in Scotland by now.

''Noelle, you go fetch a wrap and a cloak for Ferne. She must not be in the brown one you said the neighbour saw. And Nell, bring the dogs along.''

''The dogs?'' Both Noelle and Taylor said it at the same time.

''Trust me,'' Justin told them, shooing Noelle up the stairs. When she was out of hearing he directed Taylor to send for Sam and the closed coach.

''And two stout footmen, Taylor. You will remain here to see that the two hotheads stay put.'' As though he were asking for more milk for his tea, he added, ''About the footmen, Taylor, armed, I think, just in case.''

The Earl explained his plan to Noelle as they sat side-by-side in the carriage, as side-by-side as two people could get when two small dogs wanted to sit in their laps, look out the windows, and in general get more than the other's share of attention. Wrenthe squeezed Nell's hand in reassurance when the coach drew to a halt outside Dynhoff's place.

The butler who opened the door to Wrenthe's knock was obviously disconcerted to see him there again, especially with a lady who had two fur muffs in her arms. This time the butler promptly explained that Sir Rupert was not at home to visitors.

''We shall wait,'' declared the Earl, leading Noelle through the doorway past the butler. The man started to sputter, making a grab for Wrenthe's arm. The Earl brought the same arm back, then connected it with the butler's jaw, shouting "Now!"

While the butler was crashing into a side table, Noelle was putting down the dogs, yelling "Ferne! Go find Ferne! Go Jasmine, Plato—Ferne!"

The dogs took off like flying dust mops, scrabbling on the tiled floor, barking excitedly. Sliding and yipping, they raced up the stairway, Noelle right behind, then the Earl. When Noelle reached the landing, she could see the dogs scratching frantically at a closed door, trying to dig under it. Muffled cries were coming from inside the room, but outside it stood Dynhoff, a pistol in his hand.

He paid no attention to Noelle, who rushed past him to free her sister. Dynhoff's eyes, and aim, were on Wrenthe, still on the stairwell.

"I see that I have underestimated you," Dynhoff said.

"Many people do," Wrenthe replied pleasantly. "And I find that I have *over*estimated you. I thought you would be content with your malicious little pranks, like informing the Excise officers about the Armstrongs. I never thought you would be fool enough for a trick like this."

Still ignoring the girls, who were now behind him in the hallway, Noelle supporting a sobbing Ferne, Dynhoff nodded his head. The pistol never wavered. "I admit it was ill judged," he said. "Fool I may be, however, but I am still the one with the loaded weapon."

Wrenthe threw up his hands, admitting the lapse. "I dislike pistols off the field. They have a habit of going off when you least expect them." Then, looking over Dynhoff's shoulder, the Earl tensed and shouted, "Noelle, don't!"

Dynhoff spun around at the same instant the Earl jumped on him. The gun went off and Noelle screamed. Ferne fainted dead away on the landing. Then a dog's whimper was the only sound.

Slowly, very slowly, Wrenthe stood up. He looked first to Noelle who, white-faced, nodded that she was unhurt before she knelt at her sister's side. Wrenthe turned Dynhoff over.

There was blood coming from his nose, where the Earl's fist had landed, and from his shoulder, where the bullet had hit. The pistol, empty now, was still in his other hand. The Earl kicked it away, to clatter down the stairs. Sam and the footmen, guns drawn, stepped aside.

"Everything all right then, governor?" Sam called up. "The ladies?"

"Miss Ferne is upset, but she appears unhurt. We'll be down in a moment."

"Right. What about the chap down here? He's out cold. Should I tie him up?"

"No, you'd better try to revive him. It looks like his master is going to need the surgeon."

Dynhoff was moaning now, as the Earl opened the man's jacket and tore his bloody shirt loose from the wound. Wrenthe undid Sir Rupert's neckcloth and made it into a pad. Pressing this firmly in place to slow the bleeding, he told the other man to shut up.

"You got less than you deserve, you swine, and a lot less than you'll get if I ever see you in England again. Listen well and do not doubt what I say for an instant: Even your friends at Carlton House won't help you—the Prince would never have such an odour near him. If ever, ever, I say, I hear one word of the incident, one mention of Miss Armstrong's name, I'll hound you till kingdom comes. You won't enjoy a minute's peace.

"You have one day to settle your affairs and leave. Don't think you can just skulk off to the country either, Dynhoff. I'll have men watching. You are an insult to England, and you will be gone. Is that clear?"

Dynhoff made no answer, not even looking at the Earl, who pressed a little harder on the wound. Wincing, Dynhoff nodded.

"I'll be gone . . . my word on it."

"Your word, hah! You'll be gone or you'll be dead!"

Wrenthe stood and walked towards Noelle. Ferne was on her feet now, trembling. Noelle draped her blue pelisse over Ferne's shoulders, then took her hand. With the Earl supporting Ferne's other side, they slowly moved past Dynhoff and down the stairs, the dogs following right behind to the carriage, where Ferne cried on Noelle's shoulder the whole ride home.

Aunt Hattie and Cook were almost the only two members of the household not in the hall when the carriage drew up in Chauncey Square. Ferne walked very properly up to the door at Noelle's side, for Lady Bromley's benefit, then threw herself into Adam's arms in the entranceway. Moira ran out to discover Sam's part in the heroics, and Janie just stood, wide-eyed, until Taylor sent her to tell Cook to put up tea. Taylor himself cleared his throat a few times, then wiped what must have been a speck of dust from his eyes after solemnly shaking the Earl's hand. He tried to herd everyone into the Chinese room while Win was demanding details from Wrenthe and Noelle.

"He actually pulled a gun on an unarmed man? That's despicable! What a dirty dish the man is!"

"Win, he abducted your sister!" Noelle exclaimed, trying to take the chill from her hands in front of the fire. "The devil alone knows what he was planning to do with her, and all you care about is a minor question of honour!"

"Pooh, she ain't hurt. . . . And you downed the butler with a crosscut, Justin? Good show!"

"I only wish I'd got my hands on him." Adam came nearer, one arm still around Ferne. "But you have my gratitude, Justin, it goes without saying." He held a hand out to grasp the Earl's.

Wrenthe just smiled and told Adam that he could be the knight in shining armour anytime, for Wrenthe was dashed tired of all these "alarums and excursions."

"In fact," he said, "I can think of one way to ensure that this type of thing never happens again and I, for one, wish you would get on with it. I haven't had a moment's peace since I laid eyes on the girl." Adam smiled back in understanding, leading Ferne out of the room. Wrenthe looked at Noelle and told her, "I have a lot better things to do with my time." She blushed.

Justin took her hand but turned to Win, who was shadow-sparring in circles around Taylor, to that man's disgust. "Win, why don't you go see to the horses?"

"Oh, Sam'll take care of them. Come on, show us how you laid Dynhoff out."

Exasperated, the Earl said, "Winston, I suggest you go walk one of the dogs, or go tie your cravat, or go to hell in a handbasket. In other words, you clunch, take a damper!"

By now Noelle was bright scarlet. Win looked at her, then at Wrenthe, then grinned. "Now that you mention it, I believe I missed lunch. Maybe Cook'll fix something for me. Coming, Taylor?"

Wrenthe made sure the door was closed behind them. He even turned the key in the lock.

"That was very high-handed of you, my lord," Noelle said, looking at her feet.

"If you think that was high-handed, wait till you see what's next." Wrenthe raised her face to his and kissed her, a long, tender, breath-sharing kiss. Then he lifted her in his arms and carried her to the sofa, which was lucky, for her own legs would never have supported her. He sat, with her still in his arms, and kissed her again.

"I have been waiting forever for that, dearest Nell."

"Why?" she asked from her cloud in heaven.

"Why have I been waiting to kiss you? For a hundred reasons, Nell, but mainly because I love you more than I ever thought possible. Do you love me too, darling girl? Please say you do."

"Of course I do, Justin, more than I thought possible, too." She giggled. "But silly, why did you wait forever? I've been waiting for *months!*"

"I had to go fetch the ring in Wiltshire, then have it cleaned, before I could ask you to marry me."

Noelle thought about that, then told him, "You know, Justin, for such a smart man, you are remarkably goosish! I would have worn a string, and been proud of it, had it meant you loved me."

"Not *my* bride. I wanted to do it the right way."

"Do you *always* do everything properly?"

For answer he kissed her again, very thoroughly. "There, wasn't that done properly?"

Noelle dimpled up at him. "Very improper, actually, my

lord. Taking liberties with a single lady who is unchaperoned . . . "

"Minx." He fumbled in his pockets, not an easy thing when there is a lady on your lap, her arms around your neck, her teeth nibbling on your ear. At last he had the box and opened it. While Noelle was exclaiming over the ring's beauty, he asked, "How soon will you marry me, Nell? I don't think I could bear it if you wanted a long engagement."

She appeared to be deep in contemplation, he thought, estimating the time for trousseaus and all the arrangements for a wedding at St. George's, Hanover Square. Then: "Well, I should like to change my gown and repowder my face . . . will twenty minutes be too long?"

"You precious ninny! No Gretna Green marriages for the future Countess of Wrenthe! I have an uncle who's a bishop; I'll speak to him in the morning about special licences and things, but Noelle . . ." he whispered into her hair.

"Hmm?"

"Promise me you won't cover up your freckles anymore. I intend to spend the first week of our honeymoon counting every last one."

He was running his fingers lightly across her cheeks, down the straight line of her nose, when "Ferne!" she yelped. "I can't just go off and leave her!"

"I thought we'd gone rather longer than usual without that tiresome chit in the conversation."

"But I thought you liked her! In fact, I . . . I once thought . . ."

"That I would make her a perfect husband! Gudgeon, I most likely would have throttled her before the wedding breakfast. I do like her, as a sister, mind, but it is you I want to marry, not the whole blasted family!" When she started to sputter with indignation, Justin put his fingers over her mouth, then smiled when she kissed them.

"Hush, Nell. I have had all week to think things out, not all of the details, of course, and not knowing your wishes, but would you mind a short honeymoon, say a month, in Wiltshire? It is so beautiful, and I cannot wait to show it to you. For so short a time, Win and Aunt Hattie and Adam ought to be able to keep Ferne out of trouble, if we pack them all off to Derbyshire. Then we could all come back to London, or meet in Derbyshire, wherever you choose, and get her married off in style, and let Adam deal with her. Poor man. Then we could travel abroad or anywhere you wanted to visit, like—''

''But Win, and Aunt Hattie and the dogs! And what will your mother say?''

He sighed in resignation. ''Mother will be delighted. It is what she's schemed about ever since meeting you. In fact, I'm sure she'll be so pleased, she will give us that flea hound Diogenes as a bridal gift. . . . And darling, you can have as many dogs as your heart desires, all sizes, shapes and colours, but none of them, not one furry beastling, sleeps in your bed. That is my place, and I won't share!'' He chuckled at how her cheeks grew warm, then he continued:

''Now where were we? Ferne, Adam and the dogs are accounted for, Winston has been chafing to get back to Derby to his hogs and a chit named Sally, or is it his girls and a pig named Molly? Either way, he'll do just fine without us. And Aunt Hattie, well, she will always have a home waiting wherever we are, and I am sure with Ferne and Win too, so she will have her pick. I think she will decide to pay a long visit to my mother, though, Nell, once everyone is settled. They've already talked about it, and Mrs. Deighton is enthusiastic about helping with the children. Of course, that is only until she has grand-nieces and grand-nephews to sew booties for!''

Noelle relaxed against the Earl's broad chest, almost purring. ''I knew you could take care of everything,'' she said.

''Especially you, dear heart. The only detail remaining is the house. What shall you want to do with it?''

''Aunt Sylvia's town house? Oh dear, I don't know. I suppose I could give it to Ferne and Adam as a wedding gift, but I doubt they'll leave the country enough to use it.''

''And there is so much room at the Grosvenor Square house, where they would always be welcome. Win, too, anytime he wants to show his bride the Town.''

''That's so kind, especially when you did not wish to marry

the whole family! I once thought of turning the house into a home for unwed mothers, just to spite Aunt Sylvia, but your mother thinks it is so much healthier for babies to be in the country air . . .'' She giggled. "I know what to do with the house! I'll give it to Taylor to start his gambling parlour in!''

The Earl laughed, too. "And think how Lady Bromley will enjoy her new neighbours! It is just the thing. So now if everyone is taken care of and we are finished with all the tiresome details, I would like to go back to being a lazy gentleman, saving my energy for all the really important things in life.''

"Like running the government and handling all your estates?''

"No, precious, like this,'' he said, pressing his lips to hers.

And the only sounds were cracklings from the fire, and a thumping, as a little white dog, asleep near the hearth, wagged its tail in its dreams.

AVON REGENCY ROMANCES